A Family in the Making
Marcy Froemke

Love Inspired®

Published by Steeple Hill Books™

STEEPLE HILL BOOKS

ISBN 0-373-87112-0

A FAMILY IN THE MAKING

Copyright © 2000 by Marcy Stewart Froemke

Visit us at www.steeplehill.com

Printed in U.S.A.

Nay, in all these things we are more than conquerors through him that loved us.

—*Romans* 8:37

For my very special mother,
Bess Stewart,
with love and gratitude

And with special thanks to
Rosserlyn Andersen, Office of Adoptions,
and
Anne Bagley, Family And Children's Services
Division, Department of Human Resources,
Atlanta, Georgia

"I'm not naive, Michael. It's just…"

Still standing, she leaned her arms on the back of the chair. "Some marriages seem to be made in heaven. Both husband and wife love each other intensely, and their hearts and minds are one—on the important issues at least. Together, the man and woman are much more than they ever would have been apart. I don't want anything less than that, but I've seen how rarely it happens. That's why I don't plan on getting married. But I can have a full and happy life loving other people's children."

There was a deep and painful history behind her words, Michael realized, and he felt slammed by sudden empathy. How had she survived with her tender spirit intact?

But she hadn't—not entirely. At the center of her heart, a hurting little girl lay hidden. A girl who believed she wasn't worthy of love.

Books by Marcy Froemke

Love Inspired

A Family Man #68
A Family in the Making #106

MARCY FROEMKE

A native of Winter Haven, Florida, this author wrote her first "book" in fourth grade and bound it in hardcover—the front and back exteriors of a box of tissues. More novels followed throughout elementary school and junior high, when her love for writing fell prey to the demands of school and careers as elementary school teacher, music specialist, piano teacher, church organist/pianist and piano tuner. Only after receiving her master's of music degree did she return to her first love: fiction.

Marcy has written novels and novellas for inspirational and Regency markets, as well as having written nonfiction magazine articles. In addition, she currently serves as Assistant Professor of Education at Bryan College in Southeast Tennessee. She lives on a hill overlooking that college with her husband, Ken, with whom she recently celebrated their twenty-fifth wedding anniversary. In writing for Love Inspired, she hopes to communicate through laughter and tears the greatest of all love stories: the one between God and man.

Chapter One

❦

"You're not quite what I was expecting, Ms. Weston."

Brynn gazed at the man behind the desk and tried not to look desperate. She had to get this job; she just *had* to. But she saw nothing in Michael Hudson's gray eyes to give her hope. Only a faint hint of disapproval.

"I realize the ad in the paper asked for someone mature," she said quickly, "but I believe I *am* mature. And I'm experienced with young children. I worked part-time in a day care all through college, and during the summers I've counseled at youth camps for quite a few years."

She cleared her throat, noticing for the first time in her life how young she sounded, how eager. She could see she wasn't convincing the impressive architect interviewing her. In spite of his casual clothing—he was wearing a wool sweater, white shirt and khaki pants—he seemed formal. His manner *was* formal for someone sitting in the study of his own home. It was almost as if he were trying to intimidate her.

If he only knew, this room alone made her feel like a farm girl on her first visit to the city. Ten-foot-high walls were lined with glowing, warm wood. Bookshelves supported hundreds of leather volumes. A bank of windows overlooked formal gardens. Carpet, thick enough to sleep on, stretched from one distant wall to the other. Even the one incongruous element, a drafting table placed to take advantage of the sunlight, appeared priceless.

She knew people who hired nannies must earn good incomes, but when she drove to the interview she hadn't expected to find such an imposing mansion as this. The house, a sprawling glass-and-stone structure set among acres of manicured greenery, looked as if it would be at home on the cover of an architectural design magazine. It had taken all her courage to walk up the brick-paved walk and ring the brass bell.

This man's wealth reminded her uncomfortably of Reed Blake's old money and his aggressive drive for more. But she couldn't think of her ex-fiancé now, or her scalded heart would make her forget why she was here. It didn't matter if the owner of this house was rich or not. She only wanted him to hire her.

Striving to sound more sophisticated, she added forcefully, ''And as you can see from my résumé, I finished my master's degree in early childhood education last month.''

''Yes, I saw it listed, although you didn't note the year.'' His tone wasn't hostile, but he sounded remote, as if he were willing to go through the motions of an interview but had already made up his mind to show her the door at the first opportunity. ''Usually when an applicant omits the dates on a résumé, it's because they're afraid of being thought too old. I can't help thinking you did the same for the opposite reason.''

''I'm really not all that young. People sometimes underestimate my age because of my height.'' Brashly, she added, ''I'm twenty-five.''

''That old?'' Michael Hudson asked with a soft smile, his gaze returning to her résumé. Frustration knotted her stomach. He was acting like someone's grandfather, and he couldn't be past his early thirties. ''I see you've had no specific experience as a nanny.''

''No, but I've baby-sat since I was ten, and most of my training has been with kids under six.''

A lifetime of loving and helping children, she wanted to say, but then he might ask why she'd had so much experience. And then she would have to tell him that her entire teen years had been spent in a succession of foster homes. Had it not been for the children in those homes and the purpose they gave her, she doubted she could have survived the loneliness following her mother's death.

The children had kept her heart alive to love. God

had been good to her in that way, always sending her to large families. Otherwise she might never have learned to trust again. It wasn't that her list of foster parents had been brutal or harsh, but the constant insecurity of never knowing how long she'd be able to stay in one place had almost convinced her she wasn't worthy of love. When Reed came into her life, it had taken a long time to believe he really cared for her.

And look how that had turned out.

But thank God for the children and their uncomplicated affection.

A man with Michael Hudson's privileges wouldn't understand her background. He'd just think she wasn't good enough to care for his daughter. So she concluded only with, "I love young children and am usually able to build good relationships with them."

"I'm sure that's true, Ms. Weston," he said, moving her papers to the side and folding his hands on the desk. "However, my daughter is accustomed to a grandmotherly presence, and she has...special needs."

Brynn's distress at his words dissolved to empathy. "Oh, forgive me, I didn't realize she had disabilities. I believe I understand your reluctance toward younger people now, but let me assure you that I wouldn't hesitate a second to work with an exceptional child. Matter of fact, I'd look upon it as a special opportunity. They have so many gifts to give—"

"Ms. Weston, I didn't mean my daughter is disabled.'' His voice sounded tight, almost cold. Brynn's lips parted in surprise. What had she said to make him so angry? He glanced at her—not once while she sat in this room had he met her eyes for more than a fraction of a second—and she thought she saw a glimmer of regret as he continued, ''Since my wife's death last year, Jamie has had a special need for consistency. She hasn't…recovered well. That's why I don't want to replace Sue Baxter, her present nanny, with someone radically different.''

Despite the lack of emotion in his words, despite the absence of expression on his face, Brynn felt the impact of his pain as sharply as a slap. Now she understood the feeling of heaviness she'd sensed since entering the house, a heaviness that soaring cathedral ceilings, exposed rafters and expensive furnishings couldn't dissipate. And she had attributed her feeling of oppression to nervousness.

Grief lived within these walls, grief as tangible and immediate as a physical presence.

Dear God, she prayed, *please help this family. Whatever happens with the job, please be with them. That poor little girl, losing her mother so early.*

''I am so sorry,'' she whispered when she trusted herself to speak. ''I didn't know.''

For the first time, he met her eyes directly. After a moment he said, ''You didn't?''

''No. How could I have?''

Still appearing doubtful, he glanced at her résumé. ''You're not from Sherwin Falls?''

Brynn told him what he should have read on the

application, that she had been born and raised in Florida and had graduated from Florida State. When he asked the inevitable question—why had she moved to Georgia?—she hesitated only an instant before replying, "When I was a little girl, my mother and I stayed here a couple of days. We hiked the trails through Pine Park and floated on inner tubes down Piney River. I never forgot that or the beautiful old homes in the downtown district. I've always wanted to live here."

That much was true. No reason to tell him why that vacation had been so important to her. And he certainly didn't need to know why she'd resigned from a dream job teaching third-graders in a school one mile from Pensacola Beach.

A brief silence fell. Brynn became aware of a grandfather clock ticking somewhere, its rhythm slower than her racing heart. The house was incredibly quiet otherwise. She wondered if Jamie was on the premises. If so, she must be sleeping. Even in a place this size, Brynn believed a four-year-old would make her presence known.

When the architect finally spoke, she almost jumped. "You do realize the position is for an interim nanny? Mrs. Baxter has left on a six-month leave to stay with her elderly mother, who is having a number of health problems."

"That's why this position seems so perfect for me," she said, hope rising. "I want to find a teaching job, but that's hard to do in the middle of the year—especially if you're a stranger to a community. When

I moved here, I understood I probably wouldn't be able to find anything, and I haven't. Only some offers to substitute teach. But my applications are in for next fall, and one principal has already hinted that I have a good chance to take over a retiring teacher's classroom."

"I see." Again his eyes met hers briefly. In that instant she felt as if she had plunged through ice into frigid waters. Even before he pushed back his chair and rose, even as he thanked her politely for coming, shook her hand and promised to let her know when he'd made a decision, she knew she'd lost the job.

Brynn tried to display a brave face as she forced a smile and began the long walk to the door, but inwardly she churned with questions and disappointment. Maybe he had dozens of candidates with better qualifications than hers. Who knew? But with her graduate degree, she'd expected to be a contender, not dismissed out of hand like this, as if she were a little girl applying for a big person's job.

When she placed her hand on the doorknob, she could not turn it. Instead, she pivoted, her heart hammering. He'd sat back down, and his chair was turned toward the wall of windows. She couldn't see his coldly handsome, chiseled-in-stone face—a fact that fueled her courage.

"Mr. Hudson, have I offended you in some way?"

The chair slowly swiveled round. If her question had startled him, he didn't show it. "Not at all."

"The reason I ask is because I'm getting the feeling I don't stand a chance for the position, and I wondered why.'' She felt heat prickling her cheeks. "It's not that I expect to be hired every time I apply for a job, but usually employers at least consider my application."

"Didn't I say I'd consider it?"

"Yes, but you said I'm too young. If you'd give me an opportunity to prove myself, I think you might reconsider.'' She stepped a few paces toward him. "Maybe you'd allow me to baby-sit Jamie for a little while, at no charge, of course. Then, if a rapport develops between us—"

"I don't think so, Ms. Weston."

He sounded so final that Brynn could almost hear vaults sealing behind his voice.

It was no use.

As she turned away in defeat, she mentally rifled through the remaining possibilities available to her. She wasn't too proud to work fast food, but minimum-wage jobs wouldn't support her. She'd circled an ad for a day care director; maybe she could try for that. But what if they wanted somebody *more mature,* too?

How was she going to earn her living until next fall? Two months ago she'd believed such worries had gone from her life forever. Reed Blake had promised her security and love, and she had believed him. Maybe the architect was right about her. Maybe she *was* too young.

Once again that terrible, recurring picture flashed in her mind, the one of Reed embracing his beautiful assistant that night six weeks ago when Brynn had gone to his office to surprise him with a midnight snack. "Marriage doesn't mean chains," he had told her later. "Of course I still love you, but you won't own me when we're married any more than I'll own you."

Stop.

Any more of this and she'd start crying. And that wouldn't help her get this job, would it?

It wasn't fair that Michael Hudson wouldn't give her a chance. He hadn't been willing to see if his daughter might accept her, grandmotherly or not. What did age have to do with getting along with somebody?

She froze with sudden insight. Age *didn't* have anything to do with it. At least, not in the way he'd said.

Earlier he had acted surprised because she didn't know about his wife's death. Now she understood the reason.

Again she swept around. This time he was watching her, a cautionary light in his eyes. Her gaze roamed beyond him to take in the elegant contents of the room, the vast yard outside, then back to him, the wealthy young widower. She almost laughed, until she remembered how deeply the death of a loved one could hurt. He was no cliché; he was a living, breathing person who was intelligent enough to guard against young women who might be looking for a more permanent position than nanny.

"Mr. Hudson," she said in a rush, knowing she wouldn't be bold enough to keep on if she didn't hurry, "you don't think that I…surely you don't believe that I've applied for this job because…" Frustrated with her inability to phrase her thoughts lucidly, she drew a deep breath and concluded, "This is not the nineteenth century. I'm no Jane Eyre. And I promise I don't think of you as Mr. Rochester."

Something flared in his eyes. "What?"

"I'm not looking for a husband, if that's what you're worried about. Even a rich one. I *never* want to get married."

If he only knew, she thought. She would never trust a man again.

Even as the words drifted through her mind, she felt her heart curl around the edges. She almost sounded bitter, and bitterness could not dwell peacefully in a soul filled with the love of God.

It was only that Reed had seemed so *perfect*. He never missed a Sunday in church. The Activity Building had been named after his parents. Everyone she knew thought of him as an exceptional person, a fine Christian man. *She* had certainly believed so.

No, she wasn't bitter, only hurt as deeply as a woman could be. And the worst of it was, she didn't believe she could depend on her own judgment again. "I just need a job for a few months, that's all," she finished.

The architect's gaze dropped to the top of his desk. "Yes, Ms., um…"

"Weston," she supplied miserably. Was he laughing at her?

"Weston. Thank you for your candor." When he

looked up, his cool mask was back in place. She must have imagined his amusement. "As I said earlier, I'll let you know when I make my decision."

Brynn mumbled her thanks and exited, closed the door softly behind her and then jammed her hands into the pockets of her skirt and leaned against the door. Fortunately the housekeeper who had shown her in was nowhere in sight. She had never been so humiliated in her life.

Why had she ranted on about Jane Eyre and not wanting to get married? *Because it was the truth.* He was avoiding young women because he knew he'd be a target. With his money, he wouldn't have to be conceited to think like that. He could be as homely as a cockroach and still attract a certain type of woman. And homely he certainly was not.

She pushed away from the door and started across the quarry-tiled foyer toward the entrance when a movement drew her eye to the living room, which opened off the hall opposite the study. Curious, she moved past the stairway and beneath the room's beamed archway. The parlor was large enough to accommodate several conversational areas, including matching floral sofas that flanked a marble fireplace at the center. The far end of the room angled into a book-lined alcove, and it was here she saw another flicker of movement that enticed her down three shallow steps and onto a carpet even thicker than the one in the study.

"Hello?" she said tentatively, angling until she saw the small body pressed against the interior wall of the alcove. Her lips aching to smile, she stepped back until the form was no longer visible. "Is anybody here?"

Silence.

As if mumbling to herself, Brynn said, "I thought I saw someone, but I guess I was wrong. I must need glasses."

Brynn waited, hoping, but there was no response.

"Or maybe it was an angel. Somebody told me once that when you see something flicker past the corner of your eye and no one's there, it might be an angel flying by."

Again quiet stretched. Brynn forestalled a sigh. She longed to meet this child who, according to the father, had not recovered from her mother's death. Even though Brynn would probably never see her again, she had a strong impulse to wrap her arms around the little girl and give her comfort. But if the child was unwilling to make the first step, she knew she shouldn't force it.

Time to go.

"I imagine that's what it was," she said, heading slowly toward the foyer. "An angel."

She had reached the second stair when a small voice replied, "Wasn't an angel."

Brynn kept her tone light as she said, "No? What was it, then?"

"Somebody."

"Somebody who?"

No answer.

"Oh no, am I hearing things now? I must be sick. Maybe I'd better go home and lie down."

Brynn heard a heavy, childish sigh, then a stirring. Delicate fingers curved around the wall, followed by a small, pale face.

"You're not sick. It was me."

Advancing a couple of steps, Brynn said, "Thank goodness. I was getting worried." She introduced herself and added, "You must be Jamie."

Slowly the child emerged from her hideaway, and Brynn caught her breath at the girl's beauty. She had her father's coloring, dark hair and fair skin, but her eyes were a luminous green instead of iceberg gray. She wore a pink corduroy jumper over a flowered blouse, and her anklet socks were trimmed in pink inside a pair of white shoes so immaculate that Brynn could not imagine they'd ever been worn outside.

"Are you my new nanny?"

How I wish. "Well, I don't—"

"There you are." The housekeeper's voice resonated with controlled exasperation as she strode across the foyer. Throwing Brynn a good-humored look, she bustled toward Jamie. "I wondered where you'd hidden yourself this time."

She took the child's hand. "Come on, dear. Time for lunch."

To Brynn's surprise, Jamie wriggled her fingers free. "I'm not hungry."

With a long-suffering expression, the housekeeper said fetchingly, "I've made your favorite grilled cheese sandwich and my special vegetable soup."

"That sounds delicious," Brynn encouraged.

"I don't want it!" Jamie cried, and ran past the startled women, paused at the top of the steps and frowned at Brynn as she said, "And I don't want a new nanny. I want Nanny Sue!"

Brynn reacted instinctively, moving closer but not too close, gesturing as she spoke. "I don't know Nanny Sue, but I'm sure she wouldn't leave you for a minute if it weren't for her mother being so sick. She must love you very much."

"No, she don't! She left me!" The girl pounded up the stairs.

Brynn fought an impulse to follow the child. She turned agonized eyes to the housekeeper, who shook her head. "Jamie's best left alone when she gets in these moods," the woman said, her expression soft.

"I wonder," Brynn murmured.

The door to the study opened suddenly, and Michael Hudson emerged, his gaze set on the stairs. "What's going on?" Surprise registered in his expression when he saw that Brynn still remained.

"Jamie's refusing to eat again," the housekeeper said.

Brynn could not remain quiet. "She seems upset about her nanny leaving."

"I know she's upset," he said. "It couldn't be helped."

He turned, reluctantly it seemed to Brynn, and made as if to retreat into his study.

"Aren't you going to talk to her?" she burst out, then wished the words back. No, she didn't. He should go upstairs and give his daughter a hug instead of frowning at her as if she'd overstepped her bounds. Which she had, of course, and any fragment of a chance at the job was gone forever, so it didn't matter what she said. She might as well speak her heart. "She needs you desperately right now."

The look he gave her would have frozen fire. "Ms. Weston, you're a stranger to this house. You don't know what my daughter needs." He appeared as if he wanted to say more but didn't trust himself to maintain control.

"You're right, Mr. Hudson, I am a stranger. But I know what loneliness is. And I know it's hard enough to get over as an adult. That's why I wonder how a child with no experience in the world can deal with such emotions without the help of a grown-up who loves her."

He stared at her for a long, taut interval. "Jamie's psychologist recommended that we don't reward her temper tantrums with attention."

"Was that a temper tantrum? I thought it was a cry for help."

She exchanged another intent glance with him. The housekeeper made a small movement, dispelling the tension.

"I'm sorry," Brynn said, feeling a folding in the middle of her chest. "I—I'd better go." Certain two pairs of eyes were boring into her back, she walked to the door and exited, leaving behind a silence eloquent in its depth.

Outside, the January sun struggled to take the sting

from a gentle breeze rippling the shrubbery and bare dogwood trees. She breathed in the cool air and began to wind her way down the brick path to her ten-year-old car.

So many times in her life when things seemed darkest, God had provided what she regarded as small miracles to get her through. That last-minute chance for the scholarship that sent her through university, for example. And then her graduate assistantship, which involved organizing a network of tutors for at-risk children and was tailor-made for her interests and needs. Some might regard the occurrences as coincidences, but she didn't.

This job had appeared to be one of those miracles, but maybe her outlook had been selfish. The nanny position seemed right for her because *she* needed it. Now she realized how desperately the *child* needed someone. Whether she was the best someone for Jamie or not, she couldn't judge. She only knew that leaving made her feel dismal and lost and even more alone than before.

Chapter Two

"**Y**ou'd better hire that girl," Barbara Cyparno said as the sound of a stuttering car engine drifted into the house.

"One pushy woman in my home is enough for me, thanks," Michael told his housekeeper. He was halfway up the stairs, intending to check on Jamie as he would have done even if Ms. Florida State Graduate Degree hadn't suggested it.

"She's by far the most qualified and you know it. That last one smelled like a garlic factory, and the one before had a nasty temper under all that smiling and fawning. I can always tell. I'm a good judge of people."

"Are you."

"Yes, and I believe Ms. Weston would be good for Jamie. She seemed to care more for the child than she did about impressing you. Besides, it's time Jamie had somebody young in the house."

"She's not the right one, Barbara. And you know I have three more applicants to interview tomorrow."

"I wish you wouldn't be so fast in making up your mind." The housekeeper ran her finger testingly along the surface of the hall credenza. "You should consider Jamie's welfare over your own worries. That girl told you she wasn't looking for a husband, and I for one believe her."

Michael rested one hand on the banister. "And just how did you come by this information?"

A door in the study led into the kitchen, and the faint red in the housekeeper's cheeks told him she'd had her ear pressed against it.

"Don't get all huffy with me," she said, moving down the foyer toward the kitchen. "I'm old and wise enough to be your mother."

Michael continued up the stairs and down the hall that led to his daughter's room. In spite of what Barbara thought, his concerns about hiring a young woman weren't quite so simplistic as fearing a gold digger. It didn't take a character expert to believe Brynn Weston was genuine. Either that or she was the best liar he'd ever seen.

I never want to get married, she had said. He couldn't help being curious at the intensity of her statement. A girl like her must have had plenty of chances. Petite with short blond hair and a wide, dazzling smile, she had a gamine quality that must have driven the fraternity boys crazy.

If she wanted to avoid matrimony, she couldn't have found a better place. There was no danger of him pursuing her, pretty smile or not. After what had happened to his wife, after all the thousand ways he had failed her, he didn't deserve the love of another woman. And he certainly didn't merit happiness.

He still couldn't help wondering what made Brynn so adamant about not wanting marriage. But his curiosity didn't matter; his daughter did. Better that Jamie spend half a year with someone adequate and unexciting than to become attached to an employee much closer to her mother's age, someone Jamie might learn to love. Someone she would have to lose. Again.

His daughter's door was ajar, the room silent behind it except for a faint clicking noise. He pushed the door wider, his gaze running past the framed picture of Jamie and her mother on the desk, the white canopied bed—how Genna had agonized over its selection; he remembered her weeks-long indecision every time he entered the room—to the wide window seat, where Jamie sat plunking together pieces of her construction block set. She did not lift her eyes as he approached.

"What are you making?" he asked, sitting in the rocking chair beside the window.

"Nothing."

"Looks like a bridge to me."

"It's *nothing*, I said." After a fractional pause, Jamie pressed downward on the arch, then grimly began jerking the remaining pieces apart.

"Jamie," he whispered, and placed his hands over hers. She snatched free and with wild movements scattered the segments to the floor. Just as she started to run away, he caught her to him. For a moment she stiffened and fought, but then he felt her head press against his chest. As she wept, he held her, wiped her tears with his handkerchief and murmured comforts that he knew were meaningless. Her sturdy body was warm as an overheated oven in his arms.

"When's...Nanny Sue...coming back?" she asked between sobs.

"She's only been gone a few days. It'll be a long time before her mother gets better."

He believed in telling the truth. There had to be some absolutes in life, even if he had to supply the absolutes himself.

"I want Nanny Sue."

"I know, honey." Sue Baxter had been a stabilizing influence on Jamie during the past years. But he felt certain this outburst, like all the others, had less to do with Nanny than Jamie's mother. Unfortunately Genna was never coming back, and the child was going to have to get used to the idea. The world was a cruel place filled with senseless accidents and horrors that snatched young mothers from the children who needed them. The sooner she understood that, the better.

A long time ago he had thought differently. Make the right choices, live sensibly, treat your neighbor fairly, go to church on Sundays, and things will run smoothly—that's what he'd believed. But that was long ago, when he imagined life was simple.

Now he knew better.

At first he'd blamed God for turning away from his family, for allowing the worst to happen. After all, hadn't he and Genna fulfilled their part of the bargain, even down to reading Bible stories every night to their daughter?

He had finally moved beyond that childish reaction. There was no reason to blame some mythical God. Only one person deserved to sit in the guilty seat for his wife's death.

Himself.

Less than an hour later, Michael reversed his Audi from the garage and down the drive toward town. He did most of his designing at home, more so since Genna's death, but once or twice daily he normally visited his architectural firm, depending on need. Today a client who had hired his firm to design a two-million-dollar residence was coming to check the progress of the plans. Michael wasn't looking forward to the appointment. The client, a retiring Pennsylvania manufacturer who had illusions of Southern grandeur, wanted a plantation-style house that would put Tara to shame. Although Andrew Stetter had taken the assignment, the architect had asked Michael to come as witness. The client was proving to be a nightmare, changing his mind from visit to visit and claiming Andy hadn't listened closely enough.

As he neared the outskirts of town, Michael tried unsuccessfully to ignore the latest additions to the landscape, another fast-food restaurant and an automated car wash. Fortunately the downtown area of

Sherwin Falls remained unscathed from such generic signs of progress—for the time being, at least—but the east and north approaches to the town were rapidly beginning to look like any other thrown-together stop in the road. It oppressed him, but not enough to rejoin the city planner's board. Since Genna's death just over a year ago, he had lost interest in such things.

He took the fork in the road that slanted off toward the business district. It had been a long time since he'd derived pleasure from the carefully restored Victorians and gingerbreads nesting beneath oaks and pines on either side of the road, but today he found himself gazing at them with renewed interest.

Brynn Weston had talked about a vacation here with her mother, indicating the beauty of the town had drawn her back. Sherwin Falls had charm, all right, but no more than many well-planned Southern towns. A sense of puzzlement distracted him for a minute as he pulled to a stop at a traffic light, and he didn't notice the green until the driver behind him tapped his horn in polite reminder.

As he moved through the intersection, Michael spotted activity down a side road. An old clunker had been pulled onto the narrow, grassy shoulder, and an equally old truck faced it. Both vehicles jutted far enough onto the highway to cause a slowdown of traffic, but the situation appeared to be a simple breakdown, nothing serious.

Suddenly a young woman raised her head from beneath the hood to frown at the heavyset man beside her. She said something and shook her head, her lively cap of hair bouncing, her gestures emphasizing each word.

Brynn Weston.

Michael immediately pulled off the road, realized he couldn't back up, then angrily rejoined traffic until he reached the next block. The man who had presumably been trying to lend a hand didn't look especially threatening, but it was never wise for a woman alone to accept help from a stranger. Especially a woman who appeared as fragile, attractive and *innocent* as she. With a sense of growing urgency, Michael squared the block, crossed the highway and swerved behind the truck.

"Mr. Hudson!" Brynn exclaimed as he emerged from his car. She shivered and crossed her arms over her chest. He couldn't help wondering why she didn't have on a jacket. This might be the deep South, but it *was* January.

"Hello, Brynn," he said, his gaze moving to the man as he approached. "What seems to be the problem?"

"She's broke down," said the man, explaining the obvious. He wore jeans and a plaid shirt that stretched across a barrel chest. Up close he didn't look as old as he had from the road, and Michael congratulated himself for stopping. The stranger was probably harmless, but then again, he might not be. "Can't figure what's wrong, but I never was much of a one for engines. Broke my daddy's heart."

"Hmm. Mind if I take a look?"

"Go right ahead," the man said, as if the car were his. Michael saw Brynn's look of annoyance and stifled a smile.

"If you're all right, ma'am, I'll be gettin' on. Got to get the groceries before the after-school crowd hits the stores."

Brynn's gaze wandered from Michael's long enough to acknowledge her would-be rescuer. "I'm sure I'll be fine," she said. "Thank you so much for stopping." While the fellow returned to his truck, she added to Michael, "It's very nice of you to stop, too, but I don't want to take your time. If you have a cellular, maybe I could call a garage."

Michael was already bending over the engine. "I have a phone, but why don't I see what I can find first."

"I don't think it's anything simple," she said. He noticed that in spite of her vivacious and young mannerisms, she had a remarkably calm voice. "The car just stopped. It's not a dead battery, and I changed the oil filter last week, so it's not that, either."

Michael blinked, trying to imagine this squeaky-clean girl beneath such a reprehensible automobile. Although he paused only fractionally, she seemed to notice.

"I've learned how to do a few things," she said, sounding apologetic rather than defensive, "but not nearly enough to keep a car like this going. No natural talent, I'm afraid." Joining him in leaning beneath the hood, she watched his hands as he explored the engine. "But that's no excuse. I'm sure I could learn if I really tried."

He slanted her a look. Her face was only inches from his. As if suddenly realizing this, she straightened abruptly, hitting her head on the underside of the hood.

"Ow!"

"Are you all right?"

"Yes," she said, wincing, hand to scalp. "Look, Mr. Hudson, if you would just let me use your cellular, I won't take any more of your time."

He ignored her suggestion and continued to finger the engine parts. "There it is," he said with satisfaction a moment later.

"There what is?" Eagerly she rejoined him beneath the hood.

"Your problem is a cracked coil wire, see?"

"A cracked coil wire," she repeated, whispering. "Oh."

"It means that none of the cylinders are getting sparks."

"Electricity, you mean."

"Right. So you can't burn gas."

"Oh, no. Is it—is this something expensive to repair?" She stood upright again, this time avoiding the hood. "I'm sorry, that's not your problem. Now that I know what it is—where are you going?"

He was walking toward the trunk of his car. Brynn followed as if anxious he might take off and abandon her. Michael thumbed his key chain and opened the trunk. He was hard-pressed not to laugh at the odd combination of assertion and deference she displayed. Reaching for his emergency kit, he pulled out a roll of electrical tape and returned to her car.

Moments later he'd finished wrapping the tape around the coil. "There. That should hold for a while. Why don't you start the engine?"

Looking hopeful, she slipped behind the wheel. The engine caught. Her smile warmed him like a rising sun. It felt *good* to be useful. She thanked him effusively, embarrassing him. When he insisted on following her to be certain she made it home, she protested vehemently. But he wouldn't be responsible for her breaking down again, and he remained persistent.

After calling Andy to tell him he'd be late, Michael trailed Brynn to an old but respectable motel on the north end of town. He sensed her shame as she pulled into her parking slot and came to his car.

"Thank you again," she said.

"You've thanked me much more than it's worth. Just be sure to get the coil repaired in the next couple of days. I'm not certain how long that tape will hold."

When she nodded, he knew by the look in her eyes that she couldn't afford repairs. Surreptitiously he glanced at the peeling paint on the exterior of the motel and its out-of-date design. No one would stay in such a place if they could help it. *I know what loneliness is,* she had said.

He needed to move on, but was reluctant to put

the car in Reverse. Besides, she appeared as if she wanted to say something but couldn't choke out the words.

"Mr. Hudson," she began at last, "I want to apologize for what I said at your house."

He held up a restraining hand. "You expressed what you felt."

"Yes, but it wasn't my place. You were right. I'm a stranger and don't understand your situation. Someday I'll learn to keep quiet when it's not appropriate for me to speak."

Something made him doubt it. "You'll be happy to know I took your advice with Jamie," he grudgingly admitted.

"You did?" There came that smile again.

"I tried to talk with her, but I don't know that it did much good."

"Oh." The disconsolate expression on her face made him feel like a spoiler of dreams. "Well, thanks again, Mr. Hudson." She stepped back and gave him a small wave.

Michael stared at her for a long moment, feeling an unfamiliar surge of compassion. If ever anyone needed employment, she did.

He'd checked out the credentials of all the applicants, so he knew Brynn Weston was who she claimed to be. In the distilled light of a winter afternoon his earlier misgivings about her seemed foolish. He could always let her go if she didn't work out.

"Why don't you call me Michael?" he said. "I'm not formal with my employees."

"Excuse me?" she asked disbelievingly.

"You've got the job," he heard himself say. "Can you start tomorrow?"

Chapter Three

Excitement kept Brynn from sleeping more than a few hours that night, and excitement kept her energy level high during the happy storage of her car, the move to the Hudson residence and for most of the next two days. As the week progressed, however, her lack of success with Jamie took its toll. By Friday morning she found herself wanting to stay hidden beneath the covers of the mahogany four-poster in the luxurious bedroom suite she shared with Jamie.

But she couldn't. Today was Creative Discovery Museum day. Mr. Hudson—*Michael,* she reminded herself—liked her to take Jamie on educational outings. He left the choice of outing up to her.

He left a lot of things to her, she thought, yawning and stretching until her hands touched the top of the headboard. Brynn was beginning to think he employed a nanny simply to keep his child entertained and away from him and his work.

After getting dressed, Brynn entered Jamie's bedroom through the bathroom they shared. As usual, the child had slept through the noises of running water and blow dryer. She seemed to have an excessive need for sleep.

"Hey, Jamie. Time to get up. We're going to the museum, remember? The theme is about colors this month." Brynn nudged her shoulder encouragingly but briefly; the child didn't welcome her touch, she'd discovered. "Time to choose what you want to wear."

Green eyes slit open. "Nanny Sue always picks for me."

"I know, but you're older now. Don't you think you're big enough to choose for yourself?"

As she hoped, this lure compelled Jamie to rise. When the girl emerged from the closet carrying a pair of green pants and a purple-and-navy print blouse, Brynn held her tongue and tried to convince herself that Jamie's eyes hadn't sparkled with challenge.

While the child finished dressing, Brynn's gaze shifted to the framed photograph resting on Jamie's desk. The scene appeared to have been taken on the deck of an ocean liner. A younger, happier Jamie smiled up at her mother, whose face was turned fully toward the camera as if beaming into an impossibly bright future. The woman's long auburn hair lifted in the breeze; her translucent skin glowed with fragile beauty.

No wonder the child is depressed, Brynn thought

as she followed Jamie to the kitchen. Genna Hudson looked exceptional in every way. She must have been the perfect mother. The kind of mother I wanted to be for my children, Jamie realized with a pang of irretrievable loss.

Friday was Barbara's morning to grocery shop, so Brynn prepared cereal and made toast as Jamie swung her bar stool in half circles. When Brynn started brewing a fresh pot of coffee, Michael entered the room, startling her. He appeared just as surprised to see them, and after a fractional hesitation during which she was certain he considered turning around and leaving, he strode toward the coffeepot.

"I live here, you know." He opened a high cabinet and reached for a mug. "You've got to stop jumping every time I walk into a room."

"I'm sorry," she said, bewildered at his grumpy tone. "We don't usually see you at breakfast."

"Hi, Daddy," Jamie said.

"Hi, baby." He leaned against the counter, his gaze moving from the busy coffeemaker to his daughter.

"Can you go with us to the color museum, Daddy?"

"Sorry. I have to work." Brynn saw his eyes sharpen, and felt a stab of dismay. "What in the world are you wearing?"

The girl's lips turned downward. "I picked it out. Brynn said I could."

"*Did* she."

Responding to the accusatory question in his eyes,

Brynn explained, finishing with a feeble attempt at humor—those gray eyes looked so forbidding!—"The museum's theme this month is color, and I think she chose her outfit in celebration of it."

"She can celebrate some other way. No daughter of mine is going out in public looking like she dressed in a thrift shop."

Brynn turned her back to him. She had just put the milk in the refrigerator, and now she pulled it out again. With deliberately quiet motions she filled the cream pitcher halfway with milk, then to the top with real cream, just as Barbara did for Michael every day.

She would not say anything, she would *not*. She needed this job. But one glance at Jamie's crushed expression and her resolution failed.

"Some of my best outfits come from resale stores," she said. "Personally I don't see anything wrong with recycling. It's a great way to save money." She set the cream pitcher and a spoon on the counter beside him, then lifted her gaze to his. "And I think Jamie looks great."

If she thought to shame him, her effort failed. His eyes met hers without wavering, and he said softly, "You're not the only one who's had to dress in secondhand clothes. I promised myself a long time ago that my children wouldn't have to."

Brynn felt herself deflate. The possibility that he might have come from less-than-privileged circumstances had never entered her mind. He was so self-assured, his manner so elegant, that he appeared born to wealth. She began to burn with curiosity, but her questions weren't important. Jamie was.

"I don't mean to give offense," she said in the same quiet tones he used, "but..." Her eyes swept in the child's direction. "Could I speak with you privately for a second?"

For one heart-stopping instant she thought he would refuse. Finally, with every appearance of reluctance, he followed her to the pantry. As Brynn passed Jamie, she saw the child's eyes were round with attention, and to prevent her trailing them, she chirped, "Be right back!"

The pantry opened off the hall leading from an attached garage to the kitchen and was larger than many of the bedrooms Brynn had slept in as a child. Still, with Michael towering over her, his expression forbidding, she felt the closet walls narrowing to the size of a small box, and the cans and packages lining the shelves seemed to press inward and radiate heat.

"Since you've been taking Jamie to a psychologist," she began, trying to sound braver than she felt, "I thought you might value something I've learned in school. In my training, I've taken a number of child psychology courses. One of the famous theorists is Erik Erikson—ever heard of him?"

"No," he said dangerously.

"Well." Her face was turning red—she could feel it. He never seemed to appreciate her advice, but she had not gone to school for six years simply for a piece of paper, and he was paying for her mind, wasn't he? "He categorized the eight stages of life that we all go through, called the psychosocial stages.''

''Oh, for pity's sake—''

''And one of the important things for Jamie's age group is that she be allowed to make little decisions,'' she hastened on. ''Things like what to wear. Otherwise she might grow up to doubt her capabilities.''

''I'm giving you a salary to help my daughter look like she's well cared for and loved, which she is,'' he said, his voice no longer soft. ''If I wanted her to dress herself like a circus clown, she wouldn't need a nanny.''

''I don't look like no clown!'' Jamie declared from the hallway.

Brynn turned in agony to the indignant child, then cast a reproachful look at Michael. He returned her stare without flinching, his eyes blaming *her.* Oh, naturally she was at fault. The employee always was.

''I don't want to go to no museum!'' Jamie finished, and ran.

They went, of course. Brynn helped Jamie exchange the green pants for navy ones that coordinated with her blouse. At least the child had gotten to choose that, although the concession didn't appear to improve her mood.

Before they left, Brynn brought Jamie to her father's study to say goodbye. His exaggerated praise was ignored by his daughter, and properly so, Brynn thought.

But later on the drive to Chattanooga, she found herself growing ashamed. Just who did she think she was, telling him how to raise his little girl? No wonder Reed had called her a child in their last, ego-shattering conversation.

Don't go there, she told herself.

But she couldn't cast off her spiraling feelings so easily. As she accompanied Jamie through the bright, energetic displays and activities at the museum, she forced herself to make enthusiastic responses, hoping to stir Jamie—and herself—from listlessness.

She failed. They only stayed an hour. By the time she drove the family van onto the ramp toward I–75 south, both of them had fallen into glum silence.

She darted a look over her shoulder at Jamie, who was belted into her booster seat behind and opposite Brynn. The girl sat huddled against the side of the van, her finger tracing invisible designs in the window. Her expression was so lost and unhappy that Brynn felt her throat grow tight and her eyes sting.

Oh, God, what can I do for her? I've tried my best, but my best isn't good enough.

A verse was teasing at her mind, a rather obscure one that her mother had taught her long ago. Something about God and rivers and seeing… "He cutteth out rivers among the rocks; and his eye seeth every precious thing." It was from Job, one of the saddest and yet most triumphant books in the Bible. Job had lost everything—his children, his possessions, his health—but he remained faithful and was blessed by God.

Now, why had she thought of that?

Brynn mentally shook herself, then sent Jamie a smile. "Are you getting hungry for lunch?"

"No."

Smile fading, Brynn thought she might tell Jamie the story of Job if the girl were older. But Jamie wouldn't be able to relate to a mature man's sorrows. She only knew how much she missed her former nanny.

And the loss of her mother was beyond bearing, of course. Brynn understood how she felt. Jamie wasn't the only one to lose her mother at a young age.

Her fingers tightening on the steering wheel, Brynn saw the traffic speeding around her but felt oddly remote from it.

He cutteth out rivers among the rocks.

Her memory flashed onto her mother's face. They had been sitting on a large flat rock overlooking a stream when Brynn had learned that verse.

Pine Park.

Was this a message, another small miracle?

Only one way to find out.

"Jamie," she said, and this time her excitement was not forced, "when's the last time you went to Pine Park?"

"I haven't been there before," she said, sounding bored.

Brynn's forehead creased with incredulity. How was it possible Michael Hudson had never taken his daughter to that beautiful nature reserve? It couldn't be more than a ten-minute drive from his home.

"What would you say to our visiting it this afternoon? We could stop at the store and get food for a picnic. You and I could eat beside the waterfall."

Jamie shrugged. "I don't care." But Brynn believed she saw a spark in her eyes, and drew encouragement from it.

The walk to the falls took less time than Brynn remembered. Over ten years since she'd been here, and every step that led them deeper into the forest brought a memory.

Clasping Jamie's hand, she led her carefully downward, where she allowed the child to choose their nesting place on one of the wide rocks waiting below.

Once settled, Brynn pulled bologna sandwiches, potato chips, cellophane-wrapped cookies and two cans of soda from the shopping bag.

"This is what I ate with my mother when I came here a long time ago."

Jamie looked at her with interest and accepted her sandwich.

"You and your mommy came here?"

"Yes." Brynn bit into the soft white bread. It was so good. "She was a wonderful woman. We did a lot of things together." In the time we had.

"Where is your mommy?"

After several heartbeats, Brynn answered, "She's in heaven."

"Oh. She died." Jamie took another bite of her sandwich. "My mommy died, too."

"I know she did, honey. I'm very sorry. It's hard to get along without our mothers." An understatement if ever there was one.

The child's gaze followed a squirrel as it rustled through dead leaves and bounded up a tree. "Daddy don't believe in heaven."

"He *doesn't?*" Brynn's heart dived. She felt profound disappointment in Michael Hudson. Even if he was an atheist, how could he deny his child the comfort of heaven? "Well, a lot of people *do,*" she asserted. "Me, for instance."

"Me, too."

Jamie's eyes met hers, and Brynn's spirits soared. For the first time the girl seemed to be seeing her as a person.

"I'm glad, Jamie."

"Daddy used to believe in heaven. That's what Nanny Sue told me. But he got mad when Mommy died and he don't anymore."

"Oh." Brynn felt deep sorrow that his grief had led him to lose his faith. Some people reacted that way when life went wrong, but for her it had been just the opposite. She didn't know how she could have gotten through thus far without feeling God's guidance. "He loved her very much. Maybe someday he'll find healing in his heart, and then he'll believe again."

The girl appeared not to hear. A young couple dressed in matching shirts and shorts went past on the trail above, and Jamie's gaze followed them. Brynn suspected she'd lost interest in the subject until she said, "It happened last Christmas. She got killed in a car accident."

"Oh no," Brynn groaned. Sudden deaths always seemed harder on the families left behind. Her own mother had declined over a period of months. By the time the cancer had taken her, Brynn was prepared. Or as prepared as a twelve-year-old could be for something like that.

Jamie bounded to her feet and walked closer to the stream. "But Daddy didn't get hurt."

"Daddy," Brynn repeated mindlessly. "Your father was in the accident?"

"Yeah." She picked up a stone and threw it into the water, then turned to look at Brynn. "He drove the car."

Overcome, Brynn lowered her gaze and averted her face, a bitter taste flooding her mouth. The scope of this tragedy ran much deeper than she'd imagined. No wonder Michael Hudson seemed so aloof. Not only had he endured the sorrow of losing a beloved wife, but he must feel responsible for her death. Any man with his strength of character would. He probably felt guilty for surviving, too.

He'd wrapped himself up in his cocoon of an office, spent over a year in grief, self-punishment and gloom.

Her heart vibrated with sympathy. And more than a little outrage.

He might think he could cut himself off from the world and his daughter forever, but he couldn't.

She wouldn't let him.

Chapter Four

By eight-thirty on Saturday morning, Michael had worked almost three hours on his favorite project, a plan for a neighborhood built from the ground up. As a kid in college he'd fantasized about designing the ideal city, but as he'd grown older he'd narrowed his dream to plotting the perfect residential area. He worked on it whenever possible, rising when he couldn't sleep, or getting up early like today. Which was why the sounds coming from the kitchen made him frown.

Thumps. Pots banging. A mixer whirring loud as a helicopter. Voices and muffled giggles.

He tried to ignore the racket, but couldn't.

When Barbara cooked, she understood he needed quiet to work. But Barbara had weekends off, and it didn't take a detective to guess who was making the uproar in the next room.

After yesterday, when Brynn Weston had tried to tell him about some psychologist she'd studied in college—as if she knew anything about parenting—he was beginning to think his initial impression about her was right. He never should have hired anyone so young. But what was done was done. She'd have to adjust to the rhythms of his household, that was all. And now was as good a time as any to begin.

He crossed to the door dividing kitchen from study and opened it. Brynn and Jamie were working behind the island bar, both of them intent over a bowl. A screen of hanging pots hid their faces from view, and neither noticed his entrance. Jamie was standing on the step stool and pouring blueberries while Brynn stirred. Flour covered the countertop like volcanic ash.

"We fold the blueberries in like this," the nanny was saying. "Folding is a very gentle kind of stirring so you won't crush the fruit."

"Don't hurt the baby blueberries."

Brynn chuckled. "That's right."

Dead weight settled in Michael's chest. With their faces hidden, he could almost imagine Jamie and Genna standing there. Now that Jamie was four, Genna would have stopped worrying so much about the child getting burned or scalded, and surely by now she'd be teaching her how to cook. That's how it should have been in this kitchen: Genna, Jamie and himself.

But there he went again, wishing himself back in that perfect world that never existed, the one where little mistakes didn't bring tragic disasters. The one where God lived and cared.

Time to drift back to this world, the real one. Where anything could happen and the worst usually did. "What's going on?" he asked, in what he hoped was a neutral voice.

If he hadn't been so irritated, he would have laughed at how they simultaneously peered beneath the utensils at him.

"Daddy!"

"Oh no, did we wake you?" Brynn asked.

"I've been awake since five." He walked closer so they could look one another in the eye. Jamie had a purple smudge on her left cheek, but at least her clothes matched today. Brynn looked fresh and immaculate in a casual print dress that was stylishly shapeless. He found himself wondering if she'd found it at a thrift shop. Before sympathy started to leak away his annoyance, he added, "Trying to work."

Appearing unimpressed, Brynn returned her attention to the bowl. "On Saturday morning? Don't you ever get time off?"

"You know what they say about being your own boss," he replied.

"What?"

"I said, you know what they say about being your own boss."

She stared at him for a moment. "No, I mean— what *do* they say?"

"Oh." He laughed, then stopped himself. He

hadn't come for frivolous conversation. "Something about being a hard taskmaster, I think."

Brynn stooped and began opening one cabinet door after another. "That would depend on the boss, wouldn't it?"

"Daddy, you're spoiling the s'prise." Jamie's eyes were round and solemn as she ran her fingers inside the blueberry tin and scooped the dripping pulp into her mouth. "We're making you blueberry pancakes, and I'm making them *myself*."

"That's nice, honey, but I've already had—"

Brynn slammed a cabinet door and gave him a sharp look. Startled, he gazed from her to his daughter, whose chin had begun to tremble.

"Coffee," he amended. "I've already had coffee, but I'll need a fresh pot to go with those pancakes."

Jamie rewarded him with a grin, the first genuine smile he'd seen in a while, maybe since Sue Baxter left. And the relief in Brynn's eyes was so palpable he could taste it.

He went to make coffee, feeling gratified but also like a martyr. All he wanted was to do his work. Surely that wasn't too much to ask. And now he'd been trapped into wasting time eating something he didn't want. And if Brynn didn't stop opening and slamming cabinets, he'd—

"What are you looking for, Brynn?" he snapped.

"The griddle."

"I don't know where Barbara keeps it, but Genna used to store it in the pantry." His fingers froze over the coffee scoop.

"Oh, thanks." Brynn scooted down the hall, returning with the griddle before he'd regained his composure. "You were right," she said cheerfully, and plugged the cord into the outlet.

He ran water into the carafe with trembling fingers. He never talked about Genna, never, unless forced into it. Yet how easily her name had slid from his lips seconds ago. He slanted a look at his daughter. She was helping Brynn butter the griddle. It was good she hadn't noticed. He didn't want to remind her of her mother, not when she was having fun.

And she *was* enjoying herself, he thought ten minutes later as he forked a three-layered, buttered and maple-syruped bite into his mouth. Jamie took to his praise like a kitten lapping cream.

"Is it really the best you ever ate?" she asked for the third time.

"Yes, honey."

"I can make you some more."

"After I finish this plate, I won't be able to eat another thing all day."

"I mean tomorrow."

His gazed flickered from Brynn to Jamie. "What about brunch at Sid's?" To Brynn he explained, "That's a restaurant on the south side of town. We usually sleep late on Sundays and go there for our main meal."

"I'm going to church with Brynn," Jamie said.

His eyes locked with the nanny's.

"If that's all right with you," Brynn said hastily. "I told Jamie we'd ask you about it."

"What kind of church?" He hoped she wasn't overly religious. That would be another complication he didn't need. He and Genna had taken Jamie to various churches occasionally, but they'd never become involved in a particular one. Too time consuming, and he didn't want his daughter growing up with a load of guilt like he had.

"I've been attending Cedar West Bible since I moved here. It's not large, but they have a children's program that seems very good."

"I know the church. I've lived here all my life." He sipped his coffee and stared through the bay windows of the breakfast alcove. A robin and a bluejay were pecking at the bird feeder, their small heads bobbing like pistons. "I don't have anything against her going. Most churches are harmless and even do some good. I just don't want her indoctrinated like I was."

"Indoctrinated?"

He leaned back and stretched his legs. "My mom dragged my brothers and me to church twice and sometimes three times a week until I was a teen. By that time I was involved enough in youth activities to attend fairly regularly on my own. I never had a chance to form my own opinion about—" he glanced at Jamie, who was dragging her fork through a pool of syrup with a nonchalant air that told him she was listening to every word "—spiritual matters. I accepted everything the church and my mom taught at face value."

Jamie began to hum quietly. Brynn remained silent for a moment, then said, "Was that so bad?"

"It's bad when you follow something blindly without knowing why or thinking it through."

"I agree with that, but..." She rose and brought the coffeepot over to refresh their cups. He suspected she did it to gather her thoughts, but the action made his own scatter. Her hands looked very graceful as she poured. "It sounds as if your mother was doing what she felt was best for you. Isn't that one of the things parents do? Pass their values down to their children?"

"Ethics, yes. Spiritual values, no. That's too personal a decision to make for someone else."

Quiet fell as Brynn returned to her seat. From the corner of his vision Michael saw the perplexity on her face and felt strangely vindicated, yet oddly ashamed.

"So can I, Daddy? Can I go to church with Brynn?"

He glanced from one hopeful pair of eyes to the other. Only an ogre would deny such an appeal.

"I don't see why not," he said. "I haven't heard anything bad about Cedar West."

Jamie clapped her hands and said eagerly, "You come, too."

He pushed back his chair. "Oh, no. There I have to draw the line. I'll tell you what, though. Since we'll miss the brunch hours at Sid's, why don't I get takeout for the three of us?"

When Brynn protested that she would be fine on

her own, he said, "If you're going to bring her to church on your day off, it's the least I can do."

"You make it sound like I'm working. I *want* to take Jamie."

Although his daughter didn't acknowledge this comment, Michael saw her eyes sparkle as she traced her finger around the edge of her plate. He felt uneasy. She was thawing toward her nanny more quickly than he'd expected. He wanted his daughter to be happy, but she'd better not get too attached. Vulnerability to another person led to pain, as sure as sundown led to night.

And he didn't want his daughter to be hurt, ever again.

He'd enjoyed himself, Brynn thought later as she returned to her room to find her cardigan. He might have been reluctant to join them for breakfast at first, but he did actually sit still and enjoy his daughter's company for a half hour. She drew encouragement from that, even as she fought despair over his words.

His voice had been smooth, his words flowing as freely as a placid stream. But underneath she sensed a deep rift inside, an alienation from God and others—even his own daughter—that cut unnaturally strong. She wanted to help him, but didn't know how.

God did, though. He would make a way for Michael.

"Got my jacket," Jamie said, entering the bedroom via the bath. "Are we going now?"

"If your dad says it's okay."

"Oh, I went shopping with Nanny Sue lots of times."

Yes, but not for jeans, Brynn thought. Brynn had searched Jamie's closet and looked in every drawer for something sturdy, something more suitable for hiking and outdoor play than her expensive, color-coordinated outfits. Over the past week she'd actually begun to wonder if Barbara threw out the child's clothes at the first signs of stain or wear. Then Jamie told her she seldom played outside. Nanny Sue had taken her for daily walks through the neighborhood, but that was about it.

She thought it was a shame. Every child deserved the chance to rough-and-tumble with other kids and get dirty. She hoped Michael wasn't the type of dad who wanted to keep his little girl in a glass cage.

Steeling herself for possible failure, Brynn grabbed her purse and walked downstairs with Jamie. When she came to the study door she hesitated, looked into the child's expectant eyes, then knocked with far more confidence than she felt.

"Yes," Michael said, his voice inflecting in the distant tones of someone who is very busy and can't be bothered. She couldn't help feeling annoyed. The doorbell hadn't rung. He had to know it was his daughter out here, or herself with concerns about his daughter. What could be more important than that?

"We'd like to go to the mall for a while, if that's all right with you," she said, entering without apology.

His gaze rose slowly from the drafting table. "Of course. You don't have to ask permission to do things like that, Brynn. The van keys are always on the pegboard in the pantry. Just leave a note at the kitchen desk so I'll know where you are."

In other words, don't interrupt me, she interpreted with some resentment. "I thought we might do some clothes shopping."

He glanced from Brynn to Jamie and back again, then shrugged. "No problem. Barbara gave you a credit card, didn't she?"

"Yes, but I thought I should ask—"

"I'm getting some jeans," Jamie said.

"Jeans?" His eyes grew vague, as if he didn't know what the word meant.

"She needs something that can stand up to outside play," Brynn said in a defensive rush. "There's a nice playground near the center of town, and Jamie tells me she's only been there once or twice. I'd like to take her there this afternoon, and—"

"Sure, that's fine," he said, holding up his hand to stop her. "I've often thought that would be a good place for her to go, but Sue and Barbara didn't like the noise."

And what about you? Couldn't you have taken her? Brynn thought.

"Mommy said there was germs," Jamie said, one hand going to her mouth.

Michael's gaze flew to his daughter, the instant, ravaged look in his eyes dissolving Brynn's irritation.

He quickly masked the expression by glancing down at his work, making her feel even more sad.

"That's okay, baby," he said. "She was worried about germs because you were so little, but you're bigger now. You'll be all right."

Jamie's fingers dropped. "You still full from eating all my pancakes?"

"Still full." His smile grew distant. He looked again at his design, didn't glance up.

Brynn motioned for Jamie to leave, but the child ignored her, walking farther into the room. "You think it hurts the blueberries when I eat them?"

"No, I'm sure they like it. Now hurry along, Jamie. You know I have to work."

The child showed little reaction, but she suddenly seemed so small and vulnerable that Brynn heard herself saying, "Could you show us what you're working on?"

Chilly gray eyes rose. "I don't imagine my designs will mean much to you."

Refusing to be intimidated, she smiled. "You're right. I don't know much about architecture, but I do find it fascinating." Reed had wanted to build a house as soon as they were married, and Brynn had spent the past six months poring over plan books and touring open-home shows. Pushing away the sour thought, she added, "And I'm sure Jamie would like to understand what's keeping her father so busy."

"Can I see, Daddy?"

With every sign of strained patience, he waved

them over and began explaining about his design for a neighborhood. As he spoke, his enthusiasm grew.

"You're not using a computer," she said when he stopped to make a correction on one of his measurements. "I thought there was a lot of software now for architects."

"Sometimes I use software, but I prefer the old-fashioned way. Did I show you the shopping area? There's only a few stores, but enough to prevent having to drive into town for those last-minute things. It's in the center of the village green here, see? The shops are joined town-house-style with differing facades."

He was a visionary, she realized.

And then, before she could stop herself, she blurted out, "There aren't any driveways."

She could have kicked herself. Being critical was hardly the way to help him open up to his daughter. But how could an established architect forget something so basic?

His lips curled upward. "Look again. The streets circle the perimeter, and the garages are in back."

"Oh, I see." Growing excited herself, she said, "No cars are allowed within the common areas of the housing clusters. Children can play in perfect safety!"

"Yes, especially with the sidewalks in back bordered with wrought-iron railing. There's greater privacy, too. The few rear windows are small, with the preponderance of light coming from the parks."

"All those boxes are houses?" Jamie asked.

"Yes. This is the faraway look at the neighborhood, like you'd see it from a plane." He paged through several blueprints and pulled one to the front. "Here's how a couple of the houses would look from the street."

"You've set a contemporary next to a Victorian," Brynn said. "Interesting."

"You noticed," he said, pleased. "Now, why would I do such a tasteless thing?"

Brynn studied the drawing more intently. It seemed important to get this right. "Because you like variety?" she ventured. His eyebrows knitted together. Wrong! "No, wait. It's the American way, the melting pot concept?"

"Because it's pretty!" Jamie asserted.

"You're both right. When I started to work on this I said to myself, I'm an American, and Americans are ethnic mutts. Why should I worry about harmonizing a neighborhood anyhow?"

The mischievous light in his eye told her he had worried about it. She bent closer to the drawing.

"Wait a second," she said. "You *have* integrated the designs. These windows are too modern for a true Victorian. And you've put gingerbread elements along the eaves of the contemporary!"

"Ah-hah." His grin dazzled her.

"Ah-hah!" Jamie echoed.

"I can't wait to see this in real life. When does construction begin?"

His smile faded, became rueful. "Well, that's a problem. Someday when I've finished, I might see if

I can find interested investors. For now, it's just a dream.''

She stared. "A dream?"

"Yes. Just something I like to think about."

Jamie said, "I don't like dreams."

Brynn tried to remain calm. "I assumed you were working on the weekend to meet a deadline."

"No. This is…a hobby, I guess."

His little girl was starving for attention, and he was working on a *hobby?* "Then maybe you'll have time to join us in the park this afternoon?" she asked impulsively.

As soon as the words were out of her mouth, she knew it was a mistake. Brynn's heart twisted to see the eagerness in Jamie's eyes.

"Could you, Daddy? Please?"

Shutters closed over his face. "I'm sorry, but I can't. Weekends are the only time I have to work on this." He glanced at Jamie, looked away, then back. Made an attempt at a smile. "My neighborhood could provide you with a nice future, you know," he said lightly, and Brynn heard all the overtones of guilt in his voice. "If I can get funding to build this, I'm going to leave it all to you one day."

Maybe, Brynn told him with her eyes. *But what are you giving her now?*

To keep herself from voicing the thought, she clasped Jamie's hand and led her from the room.

Chapter Five

The day was going so well until Michael shut himself off, Brynn thought later as she trudged through the mall with a maddeningly petulant four-year-old. Brynn had been surprised at the wide selection of clothing for children in the diminutive mall, but nothing pleased Jamie.

"I want to go home," the child said after they had explored only two stores.

"But we haven't found your jeans yet."

"I don't want any old jeans, and I don't want to go to any old park!" she shouted, drawing irritated looks from passing customers.

Brynn led her to an empty bench flanked by potted palms. "This isn't like you, Jamie," she said gently. "What happened to that happy girl who made breakfast this morning?"

"I don't *care* what happent."

"Well, I do." She tilted her head and put a twinkle in her eye. "You didn't go and leave all your smiles at home, did you?"

The child's lips turned downward. "Don't have any smiles."

"I think you do." Brynn lightly touched Jamie's cheek with a fingertip. The girl flinched. "Oops, sorry." She touched the opposite cheek. "Uh-oh." Traced her profile from forehead to chin. "Excuse me."

"Stop," Jamie said with a fierce scowl, and pushed Brynn's hand away.

"Aw, I was just trying to find that smile, because it's so pretty. I know it's in there somewhere."

"It's not," Jamie said, but her obstinate look had faded a few degrees.

After that, Brynn was able to persuade the girl to resume shopping. She wasn't cheerful about it, but at least she submitted long enough to try on several pairs of denims, two of which fit and passed approval. One had pink trim on the pockets, the other hearts. Apparently she was feminine to the core. Brynn entered the checkout line feeling considerable relief.

But not for long.

She exchanged small talk with the clerk as she restored the credit card to her wallet, then lifted her bagged purchases and turned to take Jamie's hand.

The child had disappeared.

"Jamie!"

Brynn ran from the store, scanning the customers

flowing in all directions and constantly calling Jamie's name. Sympathetic passersby began to ask questions and offer help.

Please God, help me find her!

Brynn couldn't believe this was happening. Surely she hadn't moved to Georgia simply to lose a precious little girl. How could she have been so careless?

How would she ever explain to Jamie's father?

In desperation she used the seat of a bench to climb on top of one of the large, high planters. Balancing precariously on its edge, she gazed down the length of the mall.

And thank God, thank God, there was Jamie. She was standing all alone at the far end and wailing.

Brynn jumped down and raced toward the child, not caring when she ran into slow-moving bodies, not bothering to be polite as she pushed and dodged her way to the girl, not stopping for anything until she had Jamie in her arms.

"I thought she was my mommy!" Jamie sobbed, pointing to a woman entering a department store. Brynn could only see her from the back, but she wore a stylish dress and had curly auburn hair. "I said, 'Mommy, Mommy,' but she didn't stop, and then I—then I saw her face and it wasn't her!"

Brynn cradled the child against her shoulder, stroking her dark curls, crooning words she hoped were comforting, her heart breaking at the depth of sorrow in one so young.

* * *

After Brynn brought Jamie home, she tucked the child into bed for her nap and read story after story, all of Jamie's favorites, all with blatant happy endings, until the girl's eyes closed at last. Giving her a soft kiss on the cheek, Brynn eased from the room and closed the door.

Without pausing even to straighten her hair, she went to the head of the stairs. Her entire visual world had become centered on one thing: the closed study door. She took a deep breath for courage, then began to descend.

Determined not to give her employer a chance to get huffy about another interruption, she rapped on the door and opened it. He was sitting with his chair facing the window, his head buried in his hands. As soon as she entered, he straightened and looked at her with startled, bleary eyes.

Brynn hadn't believed it was possible to feel worse than she already did, but her spirits plunged. "I— I'm sorry, I should have…waited…."

Clearing his throat, he said, "It's all right, I was just resting my eyes. What can I do for you?"

"You can fire me if you want." She pressed her lips together. "That's probably what I'd do in your position."

He stared. "Brynn, what are you talking about?"

His voice was exceedingly gentle, bringing tears to her eyes because she knew his manner would soon change. As it should. She didn't deserve gentleness.

"I—I lost Jamie for a full five minutes in the mall today. She followed a woman out of the store who looked a little like her mom. When she found out it wasn't, she was so upset we had to come right home. I put her to bed just now for a nap. She didn't want lunch, didn't want to go to the park. It's all my fault. I let my attention wander while I was paying for her clothes, but that's no excuse. Everybody knows you can't take your eyes off a little one, especially in a public place. I was incompetent, and I'm very, very sorry. I understand perfectly that you'll want to hire a nanny you can trust, and I just wanted you to know I'll stay on until you can find someone else. If you want me to.''

She'd hoped he would have interrupted her by now, but his eyes had grown distant. The silence lengthened, and with every tick of the grandfather clock in the hall her heart beat faster.

''So it's happened again,'' he said at last.

''You mean she's done that *before?*''

''A couple of times. She has her appointment with the psychologist next week. You'll need to tell Dr. Coffield about it.''

Brynn moistened her lips. ''Does that mean I still have a job?''

''If I fired you for that, I should've let Sue Baxter go, too.'' He smiled briefly. ''Just don't let it happen again.''

''I won't.'' She knew her grin must look foolish, but she couldn't help it. ''Thanks.''

She moved toward the door, then hesitated. ''May I ask you a difficult question? Did Jamie attend her mother's funeral?''

"No." The shutters went down again. She could be talking to a statue for all the expression in his face.

"I suppose she was too young...."

"Very much so. Look, I know where you're going with this. You think Jamie sees her mother in crowds because she hasn't accepted her death, and you're right. It's very difficult for a small child to understand the finality of death, let alone accept it. It's difficult for an *adult*. But we talk about it. She'll adjust as she gets older." He grunted. "What other choice does she have?"

The grim edge in his tone signaled more than concern for his daughter. *He* hadn't adjusted to Genna's death, either.

Brynn closed the door behind her and breathed a prayer for help. If it weren't for her faith, she could easily drown in the grief of this household. How she longed to lighten their pain, but everything she tried seemed to backfire.

She was sure of one thing, though. She couldn't give up.

Shortly after noon on Sunday, Michael pulled his Audi into the garage only seconds before Brynn and Jamie arrived in the van. He grabbed the sacks of takeout from the front seat, walked to the kitchen entrance and paused until they exited, both of them looking pretty in their Sunday dresses.

Brynn had curled her hair, he noticed, and it framed her small face and delicate features perfectly.

Tearing his eyes away, he saw that she had taken pains to arrange Jamie's hair, too, and had tied a pink ribbon in his daughter's curls, to match her dress.

"Good timing," he said with enthusiasm, and held the door open for them. He was determined to pull Jamie from the despondency she'd fallen into yesterday. Her darknesses troubled him much more than his own, because of Genna's bouts with depression. He knew such things were heritable. "How was church?"

"It was okay," Jamie said as she passed by him into the kitchen.

"I think she made some new friends in her Sunday school class," Brynn said, following her. "Umm, something smells good."

"Fresh sandwiches from Sherwin Falls' finest delicatessen," he bragged, and set the bags on the island counter. "Ham and provolone on rye, tuna on wheat, a couple of Reubens and assorted salads for your pleasure, ladies."

"Sandwiches!" Jamie said, absorbing his mood like a blotter. It frightened him, this power he had over her emotions. "Let's go on a picnic at the park!"

His heart sank. "That would be nice, but I have to meet with Andy at the office this afternoon. Barbara will be back in case you want to go out, Brynn." He looked away from Jamie's disappointed eyes and found himself explaining to Brynn, "One of my architects is continuing to have trouble with a client and wants me to look over his revamped design. We're going to lose the contract if we don't satisfy him quickly.''

The nanny was apparently too busy unwrapping sandwiches to acknowledge him. He glanced back at Jamie and saw the stubborn set of her chin. He didn't want the day to be spoiled, and they were making him feel like some uncaring clod out of a Dickens novel.

''But we'll go on a picnic soon, how's that?''

Jamie squinted. ''You promise?''

''Cross my heart.''

Brynn's eyes pierced his. ''When?'' Before he had time to think, she fired, ''How about next Saturday?''

Talk about manipulation. He opened his mouth to protest that he needed to work, but found himself saying, ''Sure.''

In spite of the sense he'd been led like a sheep, Brynn's smile warmed him. ''And in the meantime,'' she said, ''why don't we eat lunch on the terrace?''

To Michael's relief, this idea went over well with Jamie. He helped Brynn slice sandwiches and pour sodas for the move, and within minutes they were seated at the picnic table outside the kitchen and beside the pool, which always looked sad to him when covered for the winter. It had been a long time since the wrought-iron grouping had been put to use, and Brynn folded towels over the seat cushions to protect their clothes. The day was a little breezy and he suspected his companions were cold, but no one said anything about it.

Women. They made him want to smile. At least, these two did.

As they began to eat, Jamie seemed more talkative than usual as she described her morning's experiences. She'd met a girl named Candy in Sunday school, and the story about Jonah and the whale had been interesting. Michael listened with wavering attention until she said, "I want to do love meals, Daddy."

"You want to do what?"

Brynn lifted a finger and smiled awkwardly as she struggled to finish a bite of macaroni salad. "Loving Meals. It's an outreach ministry of the church to the elderly. On weekdays, volunteers cook a nutritious lunch at the church, and other volunteers take the meals to shut-ins."

"It's food for grandmas and granddaddies so they don't starve to death and die," Jamie added.

"If it's all right with you," Brynn said swiftly. "We'd just sign up for one day a week. Each volunteer serves only five families, so it wouldn't take that much time."

What next? he found himself thinking with a flicker of resentment. This was what came of having a young nanny, he guessed. So much energy, so many ideas. He was beginning to dread hearing the words *If it's all right with you.*

Not that there was anything wrong with volunteering. Loving Meals sounded like a needed program, and he believed in community service. He'd been involved in a few things himself before Genna died. But Jamie was only four years old. He wasn't sure he wanted her exposed to the ravages of old age and infirmity. Wouldn't she find it depressing? A daughter of privilege, she had no idea how some of the elderly had to live, the terrible conditions and poverty. And disease. He could hear Genna's voice cautioning him about exposing their child to danger.

Brynn must have taken his long silence for a negative reaction, because she said pointedly, "The best way to find happiness is to do something for someone else."

"Why don't you try it for a couple of weeks, and we'll see how it goes," he said, and hoped he wasn't making a mistake.

She made a face and laughed. "I didn't mean to sound pretentious. It's just been true in my life. When I'm down about…things, helping someone with worse problems than my own takes my mind off myself."

When she was down about things. He'd begun to wonder if Brynn ever *was* down about "things," but her hesitation and the flicker of pain in her eyes made him curious. Something cautioned him not to ask. In spite of her sunny nature, she had an air of privacy that he was afraid to breach.

Chapter Six

"Okay, I think I know where we're going," Brynn said as she finished studying the handwritten map the coordinator for Loving Meals had given her. She sent Jamie a challenging look. "All set, Captain?"

"All set!"

Brynn started the engine and pulled into traffic. The first three meals were to be delivered at a government housing project designed for senior citizens. In spite of her enthusiasm for the Loving Meals program, Brynn felt awkward at the prospect of knocking on the doors of strangers. Therefore when she saw the rows of single-storied brick apartments, her determination floundered until she looked into Jamie's expectant eyes.

The first delivery didn't soothe her discomfort when a pencil-thin old man accepted his meal without saying a word, nor did the second, where an overweight woman opened the lid and examined the contents complaining, "Chicken *again?*" before accepting it.

"Old people are mean," Jamie said when the door slammed.

Brynn chuckled. "No, they aren't. Not all of them, anyway." She was grateful to be proved right when the next lady on their list thanked them sweetly and went on and on about how much Jamie favored her great-granddaughter.

The next delivery was almost as pleasant, although the neighborhood of run-down cottages and rusted mobile homes reminded Brynn uncomfortably of her childhood.

Jamie seemed very quiet as they drove to their final destination. Maybe this was too much for her. Brynn was surprised at the conflicting emotions she herself felt for their senior citizens: pity, sadness, admiration. She felt grateful they could help in even such a small way, but hoped Jamie wouldn't find it traumatizing. Especially if this was her only exposure to older people.

The child had never mentioned her grandparents, and Brynn was afraid to do so in case they were deceased. She'd ask Michael.

She'd ask Michael. That phrase kept popping into her mind too much lately. Of course, he was her employer. And she'd made a silent commitment to bring light back into his daughter's life and his by bringing them together. And though she'd been with him only a little over a week, it occurred to her she'd begun to take his responses too personally.

She still felt a flare whenever she thought of the past weekend and how he was letting precious, irreplaceable family time slip away. And when she saw the devastation that came into his eyes sometimes, her heart wilted along with his.

In a few months she would leave the Hudson household forever. She mustn't let herself get emotionally involved.

"Can we go in now?" Jamie asked, sounding impatient.

Brynn's attention focused. Somehow she had parked in the gravel driveway of a brown-shingled house. Allowing Jamie to carry the last meal, she rapped on a door rippled with moisture and wear. The wood looked incredibly flimsy; a child could knock a hole through it.

"Who is it?" asked a quivering voice.

"Loving Meals!" Jamie shouted before Brynn could open her mouth.

"Come in, honey. The door's open and my walker's somewhere but I can't find it."

"Do you think you should leave your door unlocked?" Brynn asked as she and Jamie entered a living room crowded with mismatched furnishings and a large old radio. From here she could see directly into the kitchen, where an ancient floral wallpaper pattern clashed painfully with the linoleum. Inside the kitchen a plastic table and chairs sat littered with crumbs, a loaf of bread and what appeared to be that morning's breakfast dishes.

"Couldn't nobody get in if I locked it," the white-haired lady said from her chair, a chuckle in her voice. "Not if they had to wait for me to open it."

She was blind. Brynn immediately wanted to warn Jamie, but didn't know how.

"What's that?" Surprisingly, the child had gone to stand beside the woman without her usual warming-up period. Maybe the flash of knitting needles had mesmerized her.

"What, this? Oh, that's how I make my mad money, little one. I sell dolls at flea markets and such. See those over there on the couch?"

"They don't look like dolls."

She laughed heartily. "Not yet, but you wait until my grandbaby gets done with them. He does the stuffing and attaches the heads. You want to see my grandson? Here's his picture next to me on the table. He lives with me, but he's in school right now, the second grade, and his name is Chad. Chad Boyd. And I'm Leta."

"Here's your food." Jamie set the meal on the chairside table and lifted the photograph. As Brynn introduced herself and Jamie, the child turned the frame upward, and Brynn finished with a squeak as she tried to stifle a giggle.

Jamie looked unamused.

"He has a mustache and pointed ears," she said.

"What?" Mrs. Boyd set aside her knitting and felt for her meal, brought it to her lap. "Has that rascal messed up his picture again? Oh, that boy.'' She chuckled helplessly.

Brynn felt warmed by Mrs. Boyd's sense of humor, and studied the photograph. Beneath Chad's artwork she saw an intelligent face and a mischievous grin. Not always the best combination, she thought with a smile.

"What's wrong with your eyes?" Jamie asked.

"Oh, honey, I'm—" The phone rang. "Excuse me a minute." Mrs. Boyd lifted the receiver and spoke cautiously, as if she had learned to expect only bad news from the phone. As the conversation went on, her responses became more subdued. Brynn wished there was a way to leave, but didn't know how without seeming rude.

"Oh, my goodness," Mrs. Boyd said when she finally replaced the phone in its cradle. "That boy." She shook her head. "What am I going to do with him?"

The elderly woman's cheerfulness had dissolved. Brynn felt herself melting with compassion. "Is there anything we can do to help?"

Mrs. Boyd's face brightened. "Matter of fact, there is. That was the principal down at Chad's school. I hate to ask strangers for a favor, but they want to talk with me and I don't have a way to get there. Chad's gone and got himself into trouble again. They're thinking about suspending him this time. Can you take me?"

Her voice wobbled with distress, and Brynn could understand why. To all appearances she was raising her grandson on her own. How did she do it? Such sacrifice could only be admired and supported.

Hopefully Michael would feel the same way when she told him. She looked at Jamie and saw interest in her eyes.

"Of course we can," Brynn said. "Let me find your walker."

Michael eased into the garage on Tuesday evening and checked his watch. He'd been needed at the office more than usual today, but it was only six-fifteen. Plenty of time to wash up before dinner. He glanced at the van beside him and felt his daily rush of relief to know Jamie and Brynn were safely home. Heading inside and upstairs to his bedroom suite, he heard feminine voices and the clink of china and crystal in the dining room. The sounds made him smile.

On weekdays when Barbara Cyparno was on duty, dinner was served at six-thirty and in the formal dining room. Since his daughter had reached her second birthday, Jamie had been included at Genna's insistence. Now he included the housekeeper and nanny at the evening meal. He needed other adults around him; he craved the feeling of family. Dining alone with his daughter made him relive, all too sharply, when two were three. And the nanny brought sparkle to the table with her easy laughter and sense of fun. Even if she did alarm him with her fountain of ideas.

When he entered the dining room a short while later, he sensed a heady atmosphere of excitement.

Taking a closer look, he realized that while Brynn and Jamie appeared like two little girls on the verge of exploding with secrets, Barbara carefully avoided his gaze.

Uh-oh.

Cautiously he asked how everyone's day had gone.

"Fine," Barbara said, so rapidly that he blinked. "It was just a quiet, peaceful day, really quite ordinary. But I did bake your favorite coconut cream pie this afternoon."

"Great!" he said, immediately feeling better.

"We took chicken and peas and cookies to all the old people today," Jamie said as she laid her linen napkin across her lap. "And Chad is coming to our picnic."

"If it's all right with you," Brynn said immediately.

Michael winced at the familiar phrase.

"Who's Chad?"

"He's a bad boy," his daughter told him gustily. "He poked his teacher with a fork."

"What?"

"And he called her a pig-woman," Jamie added.

Michael closed his eyes for a moment, opened them.

"Brynn?" he commanded.

She set down her glass of tea and began to talk. He was so distracted by her animated gestures and excited eyes that he heard only half of what she said, something about a blind grandmother caring for her eight-year-old grandson because her daughter had died of hepatitis and the father was killed in a motorcycle accident a month before he was born and—

"Hold it, Brynn," he had to say. "Slow down. Tell me about this delinquent you've invited to our picnic."

"*I* invited *Chad*," Jamie said. "What's a dinket?"

Brynn's smile widened. "I'm guilty, too. If you could have seen him, Michael, you'd understand why. When he walked into the principal's office, he swaggered—"

"Swagdered," Jamie agreed.

"But it was all bravado. The child was afraid. And ashamed when he saw his grandmother. She was so sad sitting there. She knits, you know—" Michael didn't know, but he nodded "—but without her yarn she kept fumbling her fingers together as if she had to do something with her hands in her anxiety. Chad went directly to her like a little man and apologized. When the principal asked him questions, he directed his answers to his grandmother."

"Did he admit to attacking his teacher?"

"*Attacking* is too strong a word," Brynn said. "He didn't break the skin or leave so much as an imprint."

"I'm so relieved," he said skeptically.

Barbara leaned toward Brynn. "Tell him why he did it. Tell him what that teacher said."

"It happened during lunch. Teachers don't usually have cafeteria duty anymore, but the aides were at a conference and all the teachers were dining with their students. Mrs. Jewell saw Chad eating his spaghetti with his hands—''

''He tried to eat it with his fork but it kept falling off, and he was too hungry to wait,'' Jamie added helpfully. ''See, Daddy, I told you sgetti's too hard to eat.''

''Spaghetti really is a problem,'' Brynn said. ''Anyway, his teacher huffed down the aisle—''

''Wait a second,'' he said, regarding her with narrowed eyes. ''She *huffed?* How do you know she huffed? Were you there?''

''I just know,'' Brynn said firmly.

''Because Chad told us,'' Jamie added.

''Oh,'' Michael said, rolling his eyes and gesturing upward. ''Well, then.''

The nanny ignored his disbelief. ''He has a remarkable way of making you see what he's describing. I think he's a born storyteller.''

''I wouldn't doubt it for a minute.''

Brynn stopped, then gave him a begrudging grin so charming that his resistance softened a few degrees. ''Let's just say that I've seen more than one teacher lose her professionalism in my life, as I'm sure you have, too. Anyhow, Mrs. Jewell grabbed Chad's arms and shook them until he released the spaghetti. And then she asked him if he was a pig or was he just blind and had to feel his food before he could get it into his mouth?''

After a moment Michael said, ''Ouch.''

''Precisely. That's when Chad lost it. This isn't their first confrontation. They haven't gotten along all year. I'm going to be a teacher, and I understand how hard it is in the classroom. I don't want to put the responsibility all at Mrs. Jewell's feet, but she *is* the adult in the relationship. We met her in the principal's office, where she recited a list of his sins a mile long. Nothing he'd done was serious, but she seems bound to keep track of every little thing. It's obvious she can't stand him.''

"I guess being stabbed with a fork won't improve her attitude any."

"No, I imagine not," Brynn admitted.

"She's a pig-woman!" his daughter declared.

"Jamie!" Barbara scolded. "We don't talk like that in this house."

Michael looked at Brynn. "But we will if we're around dinkets, won't we?"

"It's just an invitation to a picnic," she said softly, looking so vulnerable that his hand tightened on his fork. He couldn't give in on this. What would Genna have said?

"You sound absolutely besotted with this boy."

"I guess I saw—" She broke off, her cheeks darkening.

"Saw what?"

She hesitated. "There's just something about him...something brave. In spite of the disadvantages in his life, he isn't letting it keep him down. He's a survivor, I think. I admire that."

"You seem to know a lot about him from just one meeting."

"Maybe so," she said, looking playful. "You could tell me if I'm wrong on Saturday...."

They should make a movie about her and call it *The Manipulator,* he thought, caught between amusement and irritation. Why was it so hard to tell her no?

"I don't suppose there's a graceful way of withdrawing an invitation once it's given," he said.

She beamed. "Thank you, Michael."

"Thank you, Michael," Jamie repeated, clapping.

"That's Daddy to you, little girl," he told her. "And just so we all understand, Saturday is the one and only time we're doing this." To Brynn he added, "I intend to keep my daughter from dinkets as long as I can."

She was silent so long that Michael knew something was wrong. "That may be a problem," she said finally.

"Oh? Why is that?" There were limits to his patience, and she was getting near the edge.

"I told the principal, Mr. Bridges, that I would meet with Chad a couple of times a week for the next few weeks."

"You did *what?*"

"Well, it was the only way Mr. Bridges would let him stay in school. He was going to suspend him for the rest of the week, and you know how bad that would look on Chad's record. I reminded Mr. Bridges that I was a certified teacher—we'd met before, when I applied for a job at his school—and when I told him I'd help Chad with his schoolwork and try anger management techniques with him, he said fine.''

"So you talked him into it. Why doesn't that surprise me?" Trickles of irritation iced his voice. "You have no right to make decisions like that without consulting me, Brynn. I understand your wanting to help this boy, but my daughter's welfare is my main concern and should be yours, too. I'm not going to have wayward children coming in and out of my house and putting her in danger.''

A throbbing quiet fell. Michael could almost hear the blood roaring in his veins. Brynn's face had gone pale, and he found he couldn't look at her. Jamie had covered her ears with her hands.

"I'm going to get some fresh tea," Barbara said suddenly, and hurried from the room.

"I'll meet with Chad on my own time at his home," Brynn said quietly, her eyes like dark holes in a mask.

"Fine," he said.

She was very young, he reminded himself. Young and idealistic. He couldn't help being drawn to her altruism, couldn't help admiring her character. But Jamie came first. First, last and always.

All he expected was for Brynn to be reasonable.

So why did he feel like a monster?

Chapter Seven

Brynn moved through the next few days feeling out of sorts. Undeniably part of her discomfort came from hurt. Michael's outburst had shocked and disturbed her. What came afterward was almost as bad. Her conversations with him were guarded and stiff, a situation she feared might become permanent.

But the worst drain on her spirits was the growing conviction that he'd been right. Looking at the situation from a parent's viewpoint—which she hadn't until Tuesday evening—bringing Chad into the Hudson household *must* seem like an intrusion. Of *course* Michael was afraid of exposing Jamie to bad influences, which he was bound to think Chad was from the way the boy had reacted to his teacher.

Maybe after the picnic Michael would change his mind about him, if Chad didn't mess up too badly. In any case, she had to remember where her loyalties lay.

And so she stumbled through the next days feeling guilt, anger and worry while performing her regular duties.

She took Jamie to her bimonthly appointment with Dr. Coffield and found the psychologist to be a warm, sensitive man who appeared as perplexed as everyone else at Jamie's continued grief.

"She seems happier," he told Brynn as Jamie ran to play with a puzzle in the waiting room. "You're a good influence on her. She talks about you in positive ways. But it concerns me she still looks for her mother. Normally children as young as Jamie recover faster."

"She's unusually sensitive, I think," Brynn replied, and he agreed.

"Encourage her to express herself verbally and artistically," he advised.

Brynn did her best in the days following, but the child showed little inclination to talk about her mother. Sometimes she wondered if she was helping Jamie at all.

At least I'm not crying about Reed anymore. The realization brought a shock of joy. She still mourned her loss of trust, the shattering conviction that she wasn't worthy to hold any man's love, but the sharpest edges of sorrow were smoothing over.

The thought came as she was searching one morning for a favorite scarf and ran across the one photo of Reed she'd kept, a snapshot of him sitting in the fork of a massive oak. Seeing his picture brought a familiar prickling sensation, but the pain had dulled. The wound was healing.

God was bringing her through as He always had, by giving her another family—*two* families—to care for and with whom she could share her life for a while. The Hudsons' problems had become her own, and so had Chad's and his grandmother's.

She was replacing the framed photo when something struck her. Amazing how much Reed and Michael favored each other, although her employer's coloring was darker and more striking. On second glance it wasn't so much a physical resemblance as something indefinable, a certain resolution to the jaw that must come with the authority of wealth and having one's wishes granted much of the time.

She tucked the frame beneath a spare purse and told herself not to forget the insight.

By the time Saturday morning arrived, her excitement had resurfaced. The prospect of seeing Chad again demanded anticipation. Michael had mentioned something about her being besotted by the boy. That wasn't quite right.

She had loved Chad on sight.

That she could feel so strongly about a particular child went beyond her understanding. One of the reasons she'd chosen teaching as a profession was that she found it easy to love most children. But what she felt for Chad struck deeper. It was almost as if he were a relative. A little brother, maybe.

If she'd been a very young bride, he could have been her son.

She couldn't help thinking God had put the boy in her path as one of His small miracles. She was afraid to go beyond that thought, afraid to wonder *why*.

Chad didn't look like much of a miracle when he came out of his bedroom on Saturday morning. His jeans and sweatshirt were clean if wrinkled, but the scowl on his face forecast trouble. After she introduced Michael—Mrs. Boyd was painfully grateful and Chad made the grimmest of responses—the boy exited the house at a gallop, took his place beside Jamie and made faces in the rearview mirror as Michael glided the van door shut.

"Buckle your seat belt, Chad," he instructed when he slid behind the wheel.

"Seat belts are for sissies."

"Sissies!" Jamie chimed.

Staring hard into the rearview mirror, Michael said, "Seat belts are for people who want to ride in my van."

Grimacing, Chad complied, then said, "What is this thing, a Chevy? It must have cost a lot of money. Hey, there's a TV up there! Will you ride us by Nicky's house and honk the horn so he'll look out and see me?"

"I will not."

Oh dear, Brynn thought.

By the time they arrived at the playground, her employer's face had turned to stone. In contrast, the boy's chatter had, if anything, increased.

He's trying so hard to impress Michael, Brynn thought. And his excitement made him demanding. When were they going to eat? Why not now, he was hungry! Brynn fished through the cooler and found an apple, which Chad grudgingly accepted while complaining that the rich people *he* knew could afford corn chips.

Without a word, Michael took Jamie by the hand and led her to one of the swing sets. Chad flew to the other end of the playground, and Brynn, feeling abandoned, went to a bench and sat.

Suddenly a young man with dark hair and a mustache slid onto the far end of her bench. "Which one is yours?" he asked.

She smiled faintly, feeling a little awkward at his easy friendliness, though she guessed that came with the territory of being good-looking and male. "None of them, really. I'm a nanny."

"Yeah? See that one by the sandbox? The little girl with red hair? She's mine. At least on weekends. And whenever her mother takes a vacation."

"Oh. I'm sorry you don't get to see her more often." She scanned the playground for Chad, hoping her response was sufficiently distant to send her visitor the not-interested message.

The boy had reached the swing sets, just as she knew he would. He was taking a seat beside Jamie. If only Michael would give him a push. But no, Michael was looking at *her*. And now he was coming this way. Purposefully.

On one level she could hear her companion continuing to speak. But on a far deeper, more aware, plane she saw only Michael, saw the way his eyes moved from her to the man sitting beside her, then back, saw the line deepen between his brows.

Her heart skipped a beat, began to race.

If it weren't so ridiculous, she'd almost think…no, it was too silly to contemplate. She was no more than an employee to him.

He couldn't be *jealous*.

But he was giving every appearance of it, leaving Jamie and striding toward her looking like a thundercloud.

No, he was just being protective, she decided. He sensed she felt uncomfortable with the handsome guy in blue sweats and was coming to her aid. Although she didn't need his help, the thought warmed and relieved her.

Thank goodness that's all it was. If it had been that other…

And then she found it was neither.

"Andy, just the man I need to see," Michael said, and eased between them with his back turned halfway to Brynn, causing her to scoot to the edge to maintain a few inches of personal space. "You must be here with Casey."

"Yeah," Andy said with a puzzled air.

Brynn could feel her face blazing to the roots of her hair. What was wrong with her, letting her imagination run so wild? Naturally he knew this man; Sherwin Falls was a small town and Michael knew everybody.

"I've been thinking about Hoffsteader's atrium," Michael said. "I can see bricks, antique bricks, rather than quarry tiles. He's asked for authenticity, the old Southern flavor, so we should give him what he wants."

"Yeah, Mike, fine, but I was talking to the young lady—"

"Oh, haven't you two met? Brynn Weston, this is Andrew Stetter from my firm. Andy, Brynn is Jamie's nanny." Without giving Stetter a chance to do more than nod, Michael resumed his one-sided discussion about bricks and glazing and flowers that bloomed in dim light.

Well, great, she thought. Put him in the most family-oriented setting known to man and he still breathes business.

She'd be angry with him if she weren't already so angry at herself. Imagine getting all excited about nothing. It was almost as though she wanted him to be jealous or protective because that would mean he cared. But no man really cared, or if he did, not for long. Maybe some men felt deeply for really special women, as Michael did for his beautiful, tragic wife, but no one ever would for *her*.

Not that she wanted any man to love her. Those starry-eyed days were gone forever.

Jamie and Chad were making castles in the oversize sandbox. She had half decided to join them when Andy rose, said with a professional smile that he'd enjoyed meeting her, then joined his daughter at the slides.

With traces of animation lingering on his face, Michael slid to the vacated seat and draped his arm along the top of the bench.

"Andy's a good man," he said expansively.

"He seemed nice in the two minutes we talked."

"Hah. Much as I like him, I guess I should warn you that since his divorce he's become quite the ladies' man."

"Has he?"

"Well, if you didn't notice, he must be slipping. His strategy is to target the prettiest girl in the room—or wherever—and turn on the charm."

So Michael *had* been concerned at some level. She felt a little better—simply because it proved her intuition still worked.

The prettiest girl. She wasn't going to think about *that* at all.

"Thanks for the warning," she said. "But you don't have to worry about me. I'm not susceptible."

He studied her with more interest and warmth than he'd displayed since Tuesday night. "You've said something like that before, something about your never wanting to marry. What is it, Brynn? Didn't any of the guys in college or graduate school capture your heart, even for a while?"

She put her hands in her lap and stared at them. "That's kind of personal."

"Sorry, I didn't mean to be. I guess with you living in the house and taking care of my daughter, it's hard not to feel some fatherly concern—"

"Fatherly! Just how old *are* you?"

With a slightly bemused expression, he admitted to being thirty-two.

"That makes you seven years older than I am, hardly the qualifications of a father."

"The numbers may not add up, but how I feel is a different matter."

For some reason, this enraged her. "I am not a sixteen-year-old baby-sitter, Michael. I'm a professional woman with a graduate degree, and I'll thank you to remember that!"

"Whoa!" He put up his hands in a defensive posture. "Sorry."

The peace of God passes all understanding, she reminded herself. Breathing in, she said in a deliberately calm voice, "Jamie and Chad really seem to like playing together."

"Do they."

"He's being gentle with her, do you see that? Look, Chad's found a pail for them to make their castle walls sturdier."

"How good of Chad," he said idly.

She slanted a look at him. He was watching the children without expression, as if his mind had flown a thousand miles away. She endured the silence as long as she could.

"I was engaged," she said.

He turned slowly to look at her.

"Just before I moved here, I was engaged to be married. Reed Blake is everything my mother would have wanted for me—at least on the surface. He comes from a good family, he has a comfortable income and he's really a charming person, most of the time. But then, right before our wedding, I discovered something about him that made me realize I could never go through with the marriage.''

"And so you broke it off."

She nodded, grateful he hadn't asked why.

"And then you came here."

She tightened her lips into a ghost of a smile. "I guess I ran away to the one place I remembered being the happiest."

"Sherwin Falls?" His voice inflected humorously, as if he couldn't believe it.

"My mother and I spent a few days here." Her eyes burned, but she would *not* let herself cry. "Mom was the finest person I've ever known. Even though we never had much in the way of security or money, she did everything in her power to enrich my life."

"It was just the two of you?"

"My dad was a policeman. He was killed trying to rescue hostages at a convenience-store robbery when I was very small. After that, Mom worked as a waitress to support us. She must have been exhausted when she came home at night, but she always had time for me. She was so fun, so lively.

"For years she saved her tips to take me to the Grand Canyon. Finally, when I was twelve, she felt ready. We planned to do the trip in stages because our car was in such bad shape. We got as far as Macon when it died. Mom had to use the vacation money to buy another car, another old one, but at least it ran. She had a small amount left over, enough to get us to the Tennessee line, she thought. But Sherwin Falls was our last stop.''

''You must have been very disappointed.''

She shook her head. ''Not with Mom along. Sometimes we camped out, sometimes we stayed in cheap motels, we lived on sandwiches, but it was glorious, all of it.''

A large ball suddenly rolled to her feet. The towheaded boy chasing it turned shy as he neared. She tossed the toy to him.

''And then Mom got sick when we returned home. She died within the year.''

He regarded her in silence for a moment. ''I'm sorry.'' She shrugged, not trusting herself to speak. ''What happened to you then? Did you have relatives to stay with?''

''No one close. Except for my dad's father, all my grandparents were gone, and my grandfather was in a nursing home. So the state of Florida took over my care.''

''Foster homes?''

She nodded. There was no reason not to tell him about her past. Now that she knew him better, she had no worries that he was the kind of man who'd fire her for something she couldn't help.

''It wasn't bad. My placements were with good families. The worst part was getting adjusted to a new town and making friends, then having to move because of changes—like when one foster mother became pregnant and couldn't handle any more kids, or the time one of the foster fathers was transferred to South Dakota.... That sort of thing.''

"You *must* have had good parenting, because you went on to college and graduate school. That took courage.''

Though the compliment gave her a rush, she shook her head, unable to accept it. "My mother was responsible for that. She made me promise to get a good education so I'd be able to take care of myself. Even as she struggled with her illness, she accented the positive. She was a real woman of God. She taught me that good can come out of the worst circumstances, and I still believe it.''

"Do you?" His eyes rested softly on her. "Even after you were almost a bride?"

"I'm not the kind of person who feels I need to be married to have a fulfilled life, Michael. Besides, if I'd married Reed, I'd never have met Jamie or Chad.'' *Or you.* The unvoiced thought made her shudder inside. She *was* becoming too emotionally involved. It was time to step back.

Sudden screams brought her sharply to the present. Jamie was standing in the middle of the sandbox, her face contorted with rage as she ruffled a deluge of sand from her hair. Fists flying, Chad and another boy were rolling in the grass and shouting. A small circle of children had already gathered to watch, and more were flocking over. One or two parents wandered closer.

"If he's hurt her..." Michael said, and took off running.

Brynn followed closely behind, heart racing with anxiety, her ears ringing with the implied threat in his voice. The first thing he thought was that Chad was at fault for whatever had happened to Jamie. He must really detest the boy. Her hopes for the day crumbled.

"He threw sand all over me!" Jamie cried as her father reached her.

"Are you hurt?" Michael demanded.

"Sand's in my eyes!"

Brynn kneeled in the grass beside her and began to help Michael brush off the sand. Within seconds she knew the girl was more upset than injured, so she raced across the sandbox to stop the fight. One of the fathers helped her separate the boys. By the time she'd pulled Chad to the side, Michael joined them carrying Jamie in his arms.

"What happened here?" he asked, his gaze spearing Chad.

"He stole my bucket!" the other boy cried.

"You're bad!" Jamie said to him. "You threw sand on me!"

"But *he* wouldn't give me my bucket back!"

Chad's chin hardened. "I didn't know it was your old bucket, stupid—it was just sitting there. You didn't want it till we started playing with it."

"Give him the pail," Michael told him grimly. "And then we're going to take you home."

"But Chad didn't do anything," Jamie snuffled.

"None of this would have happened if Chad hadn't stolen the bucket."

The boy's face flushed. ''But I didn't steal it! I'm not a thief!''

Brynn saw the hurt behind the child's anger and felt grief. This was all her fault. She shouldn't have pressed Michael to bring Chad when he was obviously biased against him. It dismayed her that her employer had so little empathy for a child from a disadvantaged background, especially after he'd implied he came from similar circumstances.

As they returned to the van, Jamie protesting in his arms and Chad refusing to take Brynn's hand, Michael looked too set, too angry for her to ask him to change his mind, and a refusal would make Chad feel even worse. So she said nothing.

Maybe Michael wasn't ready to admit anyone else into his tight little world. Maybe his grief had narrowed his interests to the numbing drug of work, with a few drops left over for Jamie.

Chapter Eight

On Valentine's Day Barbara baked a heart-shaped cake for dessert, and at her suggestion they carried their plates to the sunroom after dinner. Michael seldom visited the inviting room with its white wicker furnishings, lacy plants and wide view of the outside terrace and pool, because it had been Genna's favorite place. But the days were growing longer, the sun warmer, and he felt ready to do anything to brighten up Jamie, who had never really forgiven him for that day at the picnic weeks ago.

At least, he figured that was what it was. She hadn't seemed as talkative or happy since. But maybe that was because Brynn's attention had become divided and her presence increasingly absent, like tonight.

He didn't like it any more than Jamie did, because he believed his daughter needed her. But he couldn't do anything about it. No employer could expect twenty-four-hours-a-day service, not in the twenty-first century.

After he sat on the sofa, Jamie bypassed him to sit in the glider as she ate her cake. Her feet didn't reach the floor, so she tried to make it move by jutting her head back and forth. The earnest expression on her face tickled him.

"Hey, turtle," he said. "Want me to sit with you and swing?"

"I don't care."

He glanced at Barbara, who raised her eyebrows and went back to her cake.

Funny how much he felt like a stranger in his own home lately, without allies, without friends. He sat beside his daughter anyway and moved the glider slowly. Best not to get her seasick while she was eating.

They ate silently while he racked his brain for something to say. The pool cover outside had standing water in it, he noticed, and a scattering of leaves. What a mess for the gardener. He felt thankful he didn't have to do that kind of work anymore.

"It'll be time to open the pool before long," he said, his words dropping like rocks into a bottomless well.

Jamie stared at him blankly. And then a vibration went through the house, the sound of the electric garage door opening, and her expression lightened.

"That's Brynn." She jumped up, set her plate on

the floor and ran to the entry of the sunroom. "Brynn, we're back here!"

Seconds later the young woman entered the room, swept in, like a spring breeze whispering away the cobwebs, he thought poetically, and wanted to laugh at himself. She hugged Jamie and went to the sofa, where his daughter promptly joined her.

I get the point, he wanted to say, but the women didn't seem to be thinking of him at all. They were too concerned with the bundles of yarn that Brynn was unloading from a grocery bag.

"Mrs. Boyd taught me to knit this evening," she explained to Jamie. "At least, I hope she did. She needs help. The school has asked her to knit a hundred dolls to sell for the PTA fund-raiser in March."

"I thought you were helping Chad study in the evenings," Michael said.

Barbara placed her empty plate on the chairside table. "I used to knit years ago. I could do a few for her."

"Can I learn how, too?" Jamie asked.

"Of course, but I'm hoping you'll also help like Chad does. He stuffs the dolls and attaches their heads."

"That's the pretty part. I want to put their faces on—can I, Brynn?"

"You certainly may. That'll be a big help."

Michael swallowed his last bite of cake. "I thought you were doing homework with the boy and working on anger management, not learning how to knit."

"I hope the PTA plans to pay her for her time," Barbara said. "She needs the money so much."

"That's the great part," Brynn told her. "An anonymous donor is paying what she normally gets at the flea market, and the PTA keeps all revenues at the sale."

"An anonymous donor?" Michael asked, trying to join in.

Brynn gave him a fleeting look. "Yes, isn't that nice? And look, Jamie, these dolls will be done in the school colors, so that should make them sell fast."

"Do a lot of people know Chad's grandmother makes dolls?" Michael persisted.

"Hmm? Oh, I'm certain they do. You know what it's like in a town this size. I'm sure everyone knows she refuses to take outright charity." Turning back to Jamie, she added, "The bodies we'll do in green and the little buttons in gold."

"Like leperchauns," the child said.

Brynn's mouth dropped. "Jamie, you're a genius! The fund-raiser is scheduled near St. Patrick's Day. We'll modify the dolls into school leprechauns, and they'll sell like hotcakes. Maybe we can make little felt hats...." Her voice trailed away as her eyes glazed with plans.

"I imagine this project will go a long way in improving Chad's stock at school," he said.

Brynn's expression sharpened, even looked a bit gloating. "His stock already *has* risen. His grades in spelling and English are going up, and he's always done well in reading and math.''

"And how's his anger? Forked any teachers lately?''

He'd wanted to make her smile, but she didn't. "He's...doing all right. At least there haven't been any more incidents.''

"Good. That must mean his probation's over, because the principal couldn't have expected any more from you. So you should be able to join us at dinner more often. Barbara's cooking is one of the perks of the job, you know.''

Brynn smiled at Barbara, who was rolling her eyes at this praise. "I *do* know, and I *have* missed her wonderful meals. But Chad still needs me.''

Not as much as we do, he wanted to say, and was glad he hadn't, because he'd meant *Jamie*—not as much as *Jamie* does. Well, all right, Brynn did spark up the house a little, and he'd admit he liked that. When she was around, things *happened.* She generated an excitement that took his mind off the accident for soothing lengths of time.

He'd almost begun to think he was recovering at last. But the dark times were returning lately, a fact he couldn't help attributing to Brynn's rare appearances in the evening.

"As a matter of fact,'' Brynn was saying timidly, "there is something I'd like to ask you. A favor.''

Barbara suddenly stirred to her feet. "Come on, Jamie, get your plate and we'll stack the dishes in the dishwasher.''

Jamie obeyed so quickly that Michael watched her and Barbara with suspicion as they left him alone with Brynn.

"Should I be afraid?" he asked, only partly in jest.

"I'm the one who's afraid," she answered, "knowing how you feel about Chad."

The glider stopped moving. "Somehow I thought the favor would involve him."

"He's in trouble. No, not like you think. There's a chance he'll be taken away from his grandmother by the Department of Human Resources, their Family and Children's Services Division, and put into foster care. The school is petitioning the court."

Much as he didn't want to feel anything for the child, Michael grew solemn. "I'm sorry, Brynn."

"Do you remember the day I told you Jamie and I took Mrs. Boyd to school for the conference—the first time we met Chad? That's when it all began. Evidently Mr. Bridges and Mrs. Jewell started talking after we left. Surely they already knew about Mrs. Boyd's blindness, but maybe seeing how feeble she'd become surprised them." Her eyes flickered. "Maybe Mrs. Jewell was ready to grab any chance to remove Chad from her class, I don't know. Anyway, since Chad is a—a lively child, they called human resources to investigate."

The boy was more than *lively*, but he decided not to comment on her choice of words. Brynn was taking the situation far too seriously for him to make jokes.

"You said there was a chance he'd be placed in a

foster home. I take it they haven't made their decision yet?''

"No, the investigation is ongoing. They're considering all the factors. Chad is healthy and well nourished, so that's not a problem. Mrs. Boyd's financial situation is improving, at least for a month or two with the large order for dolls she received from the school, and maybe the wider exposure will bring more business.

"On the educational side, I spoke with one caseworker and told her I intend to continue tutoring Chad. If he keeps his grades up at school, that'll be a strong indicator his present environment is adequate.''

He watched her steadily, trying to keep his expression neutral while his stomach churned with dismay. She planned to continue tutoring Chad, did she? That meant less time with Jamie, fewer dinners shared. He admired her generous spirit and knew he was being selfish, but he'd enjoyed coming to think of her as part of the family rather than an employee working strict hours with a life of her own that didn't include them.

And who should you blame for that? niggled an annoying voice.

"Brynn, I understand how you feel about foster homes, but are you sure it might not be the best thing for Chad?'' He felt like a traitor the moment the words fell from his mouth.

The light in her eyes dimmed. "I'm positive. Chad needs stability in his life, consistency. He should be in an environment where he knows he's loved no matter what."

"I'm not trying to downplay your concerns," he said, and wondered if he was telling the truth, "but don't you think he could find all that in a foster home, where he'd also receive a greater sense of protection as well as other advantages?"

"Of course he might find a home like that. I'd venture to say the majority of them are. But there are also some foster families who might view his personality as too challenging to bother. What do you think will happen to him if he falls into situations like that? Can you imagine him after two such placements, then three? Four? It would destroy him."

"It didn't destroy you," he said gently.

"I had my mother's guidance for twelve years. Chad's only eight, and in spite of his blustery, *I'm not afraid of anything* exterior, he's…fragile."

Fragile. How like a woman to see a wild boy and think he was a delicate flower.

"I believe you when you say what a positive influence your mother was. Still, I wonder if you'd be as caring, as strong and compassionate as you are now if it hadn't been for your later experiences."

Her cheeks darkened. "I'm not all those things, Michael. Goodness!"

"Yes, you are," he said with resolution, and realized how much he meant it. He'd never met anyone with finer character. Jamie was lucky—they *all* were lucky—to have Brynn, even for a little while.

She shook her head. "Thanks, but you haven't

known me long enough to notice the warts. Anyway, I want to do everything possible to help Chad and Mrs. Boyd remain together. If we contain the area that seems to concern everyone most, and please don't scold when I say it's his behavior, we should be fine. Which leads me to ask for the favor.''

He closed his eyes, opened them. "I'm listening."

"I'd like to take Chad to church with Jamie and me." Rapidly she added, "It's not enough to teach him about anger management—he needs spiritual guidance, too. He needs something greater than himself to give him strength. He needs God, Michael. I understand how you don't want the two children together, but it will only be in the van back and forth to church, and—"

"All right, Brynn."

She looked startled, as if she'd prepared long and hard for battle only to find the enemy had raised the white flag. "You don't mind?"

"My mother would turn over in her grave if I denied a child a chance to go to church. No, I *do* mind, but you've convinced me to try again. I want you to bring him here for lunch this Sunday after the service, and then we'll see."

"That's great, Michael!"

"Now you owe me," he said. "So you have to answer one question."

"Name it," she said eagerly, matching his playful tone.

"How much does Mrs. Boyd make for each doll?"

"Hmm?" Brynn's eyes grew vague. "Oh. About ten dollars, I think."

"I see. And would you happen to know the name of that mysterious donor?"

Smiling like a Cheshire cat, she stood and walked toward the corridor.

"Hey, you didn't answer," he said.

"You said *one* question, Michael," she replied, and disappeared into the hallway.

"I'm not paying you enough!" he called after her.

"I agree!" she shouted back.

Brynn knew better than to warn Chad to be on his best behavior on Sunday. Nobody could stand that kind of pressure, not even an adult. So she contented herself with finding a perfectly good suit in his size at a resale shop and arriving early to make sure he wore it. After he dressed and she parted and combed his hair, Chad appeared quite handsome as he entered his living room.

"He looks like an actor or a clothes model," Brynn told Mrs. Boyd.

"That good?" Mrs. Boyd smiled and clasped her hands.

"You look silly," Jamie said, giggling.

"I knew it!" shouted Chad. "I'm not wearing this stupid old stuff!"

Seeing Brynn's pointed look, Jamie said, "You look silly but nice. That's what all the boys wear."

To Brynn's vast relief, Chad calmed down, and she herded the children to the van. Church went better than she had expected, with Chad hardly protesting as he was led off to a boys' Sunday school class. During the formal service he sat so quietly she feared he might burst from stored energy.

Later, over pizza and salad in the Hudson kitchen, he initially seemed too awed to speak. His gaze roamed the exposed beams, the hand-painted tiles on the floor, the granite countertops, the top-of-the-line appliances as a child would scan a candy shop. When his eyes came to rest on Michael, Brynn felt a tug of alarm. The boy was thawing. Fast.

"I want a house like this," he stated.

Michael grunted and wiped his mouth with a napkin. "Work hard and get a good education." His glance met Brynn's. "I think I just heard my dad talking."

"What kind of job you got?" Chad asked.

Michael explained that he was an architect, then defined his vocation. Brynn wondered if she'd be able to digest her pizza, her stomach was so tense. Michael was being polite, but he seemed remote, strained, as if hosting Chad was akin to entertaining a mobster.

"An architect," Chad ruminated. "That's what I want to be."

"Me, too," Jamie said.

"And then I'm going to get me a big new house with wood ceilings and a swimming pool and a van and a *giant* kitchen."

Brynn flinched inwardly. "That sounds very nice,

but happiness doesn't come from pretty things, Chad.''

"Don't worry about it," he said, sounding annoyingly sure of himself. "Maybe some people are too stupid to know when they got it good, but if I get rich stuff, *I'll* be happy."

"Oh, Chad—"

"No, he's right," Michael said.

Brynn lowered her slice of pizza and stared. "You're telling him that material possessions will make him happy?" She hoped by saying the words out loud he'd understand what he'd implied, because he couldn't possibly mean it.

"I don't know about anybody else, but I'd rather be wealthy and unhappy than poor and unhappy, wouldn't you, Chad?"

"Yeah!"

"But you can't just find the wealth under a rock, you know," Michael cautioned. "It's no good if it's given to you. You can't steal it. You have to earn the money on your own."

What was he doing to Chad? The boy glanced longingly out the bay window, then cut a look at the hallway stairs. She saw his eyes filling with doubts and wanted to cry.

When he talked about money, he reminded her of Reed. She visualized the photo upstairs, superimposing it over Michael's face. Yes they were alike, in more ways than one.

"Yeah, but you were rich and smart," the boy was saying.

"My daddy's rich and smart," Jamie agreed, swinging her legs against the central post beneath the table.

Michael winked at his daughter. "No smarter than you two. And when I was growing up, my whole house was smaller than this kitchen."

"Really?" Chad crowed. "Wow!"

Brynn fought increasing melancholy. She'd wanted them to bond on some level, but not like this.

After lunch, when the children went upstairs to Jamie's playroom and the adults cleaned the kitchen, Brynn asked, "Do you really believe money buys happiness?"

He took his time answering, stooping to bury the pizza carton in the garbage can, leaning against the cabinets and crossing his arms over his chest.

"I was trying to encourage the boy."

"I thought so, but do you think it's necessary to give him a distorted view of the world while you're at it?"

"I don't know about distorted. A child like him understands what he sees. Give him something tangible to work for, and maybe he'll pull himself upward. It worked for me."

He seldom talked about himself, and she couldn't help showing her interest. "Did you have someone special in your life who encouraged you?"

"Not really," he said, disappointing her, for she wanted at least something from his childhood to be pleasant. "I told you about my mom taking my brothers and me to church. Occasionally the youth activities were held in the homes of church members, some of whom were well-off. I liked what I saw and wanted it for myself.''

"You mentioned your dad earlier. Didn't he give you a push?''

His short, bitter laugh startled her. "Sure. He preached to me a lot about getting a good education and working hard, all the while with a whiskey bottle in one hand and an empty wallet in the other. He went from job to job until finally one day he just didn't come home.''

She winced. "That must have been so hard for you.''

"I was glad when he left. My mom did everything she could to give us a stable home life, but sometimes he was abusive to her, and she took it. Church taught her to stay in her place, and her place was beside him no matter what.''

"Oh, no,'' she said, groaning inside. "No one thinks that way anymore. Those old ideas were based on misinterpretations of Scripture. Marriage is sacred, but a woman needs to think of her safety first, and her children's. Nothing in the Bible says—''

He held up a restraining hand. "I know, Brynn. I'm just saying that having a goal helped me provide my family with a comfortable life.''

"But did it make you happy?'' she persisted.

He snorted. "Happy? Who's happy all the time? Look at you. You smile a lot, but surely you get down, too. I imagine the breakup of your engagement was depressing.''

She didn't appreciate his bringing up her broken dreams and using them like a weapon to strengthen his argument. Tart words begged to be spoken, but she swallowed them.

"Yes, it was very depressing. Maybe happiness was the wrong choice of word." She frowned, struggling to express the inexpressible. "I didn't mean perfect bliss, but the quality of contentment, or peace, that helps you see the good when terrible things happen."

"The good," he said scornfully.

"Yes." The hurt she sensed behind his resentment made her continue instead of walking away. "My faith helps me go on instead of getting stuck in sorrow." Softly she added, "Or bitterness. It keeps me searching for meaning."

She took a deep breath. "You spoke of my engagement. The reason we broke up was…well, I found out Reed was having an affair with his assistant. When I confronted him, he told me how little fidelity meant to him in marriage. I hit bottom."

For a heartbeat she thought sympathy glimmered in his expression, but it passed so swiftly she decided she'd imagined it.

"And the meaning you derived from this experience was…"

She squeezed her eyes shut for a moment to block out his cynical expression and tone. This was not the real Michael, she told herself. Not him.

"I'm not saying God caused this to happen to me. I simply believe He brought me through it. In fact, I think He helped me escape real disaster. I could have found out about Reed *after* we were married, and that would have been a lot worse.''

He threaded his fingers through his hair, turned away, then back. She sensed his anger uncoiling and watched him apprehensively.

"You can't find good in *everything*," he snapped. "What possible good could there be in death? Can you look Jamie in the eye and say losing her mother will turn out to be *good,* when she cried for months after the accident and still runs after strangers hoping to find her again?''

Brynn furrowed her brow at the depth of anguish she heard in his voice. She should have fallen quiet long ago. He was bound to hear her words as condemnation. She couldn't settle his issues of grief and despair. Only God could.

"I'm sorry, Michael. I'm so very sorry.''

"Daddy?'' piped a trembling voice.

Both of them whirled toward the sound. Jamie and Chad were standing at the threshold, the boy appearing curious, the girl with wide, empty eyes. How long has she been listening? Brynn thought in agony. And found her question answered when Jamie raced across the kitchen to be swept up in her father's arms.

Brynn watched them, her eyes growing moist. She longed to wrap her arms around both of them, to take their pain into herself and lighten it. But she had no right. Instead, she took Chad's hand and led him quietly from the room.

Chapter Nine

"What is it, what's wrong?" Michael asked, racing into Jamie's bedroom. He'd woken abruptly, the memory of a scream lingering in his ears, when he'd heard the unmistakable sound of Jamie's sobs. Now Jamie was sitting upright in bed while Brynn held her and murmured soothing words.

In that instant he saw how trustingly the child clung to her nanny. The sight struck him with fear. Brynn was leaving in a few months. If his daughter felt this close to her now, how much worse would it be to part then?

"Daddy," Jamie cried, and stretched her fingers toward him. He sat on the opposite side of the bed and pulled her into his arms. She felt as slight as a doll. Her bones had no weight.

He had the sudden, miserable thought that the only thing anchoring her to earth was him.

"She had a nightmare," Brynn said, her eyes liquid with sorrow. Over Jamie's shoulder he saw her pulling together the front of her satin robe and felt suddenly embarrassed that he was wearing only his pajama bottoms.

"Mommy came to get me," Jamie said between panting breaths. "She said she missed me and wanted me to come with her."

A superstitious chill pricked the hairs at the back of his neck. "Hush, baby, it was only a dream."

"And when we went outside, she ran off and left me. And then I chased her but I couldn't find her!"

"Shh, honey," he crooned, kissing her forehead and cheeks, rocking her. "Mommy wouldn't do that. Dreams are tricks your mind plays while you're sleeping, that's all. Like silly movies."

Gradually Jamie's sobs lessened. Brynn slipped away, disappearing into her room through the connecting bathroom.

After several minutes more, his daughter's fingers loosened around his neck, and he tucked her beneath the covers. When he was certain she slept, he returned to his room, dressed in khakis and a sweatshirt and trod softly downstairs to the kitchen.

He wasn't surprised to find Brynn already there, although he felt a thud of dread. That she had changed into jeans and a sweater didn't surprise him, either. She must have noticed him watching her in that siren outfit upstairs, which he couldn't help despite himself, despite his daughter's trauma. Without a doubt he'd have gawked if his foot had been on fire.

Slinky white satin. Probably a part of her trousseau.

She'd been right. Nothing childish about her.

Her ex-fiancé was a fool.

And so was he, but for different reasons. That the sight of curving young flesh could still stir him when Genna lay alone and cold in the ground told him what kind of man he was.

But he knew that already, didn't he? He liked to pretend he was stronger than his father, that he could protect those in his care instead of harming them irreparably, but he was lying to himself.

Genna had trusted him blindly, and he'd failed her in the worst possible way.

He couldn't protect his daughter from the horrors of her mind.

And as to Brynn... She was a young woman in his employ, someone living beneath his roof who deserved his professional regard and protection. With chagrin he recalled his attempt to save her from the predatory nature of Andy Stetter that day on the playground. For a few minutes this evening, she'd been in more danger from himself.

"I thought you might be down, so I brewed some coffee," Brynn said in a sleepy voice. "The hot chocolate I made for myself, but there's enough for two. Marshmallows on the table. You could say I'm into comfort food tonight."

"Thanks." He poured himself a cup of coffee,

added his cream mixture. "You should go back to bed."

She shuddered. "I don't think so. Not after hearing Jamie's screams."

"They were bloodcurdling, all right." He sat opposite her at the kitchen table.

They remained silent for a while. He stared out the bay windows and saw only darkness until he gradually became aware of the clink of Brynn's spoon as she fished for melted marshmallows. He glanced from the cup to her eyes and had to smile. Looking abashed, she returned his smile and set down the spoon.

"I'm sorry for the way I spoke to you this afternoon," he said.

"No, *I'm* sorry. Sometimes I get a little carried away."

"I'm the one who got carried away. I think I gave my daughter nightmares."

"You're a wonderful father," she said.

Though her words pleased him, he raised his brows skeptically. "Really. Lately I've gotten the feeling I'm too wrapped up in work, too rigid and too materialistic for my own good."

Avoiding his eyes, she dropped a fresh sprinkle of marshmallows atop her chocolate. "You're teaching me not to think in black and white, that things aren't always what they seem."

He felt absurdly pleased and tried to hide it. "I do my humble best to widen the horizons of everyone I meet," he said. He loved making her smile, another foolish trait he couldn't seem to help.

"There's always room for improvement, though," she returned archly, unwilling to let him think too much of himself. And then she added in a woeful voice, "For me especially."

"I don't know about that," he mumbled.

She made a face. "I do."

"You've been good for Jamie."

"Hence her nightmare tonight," she said gloomily.

"That was my fault. And then there's Chad. You've managed to persuade me to let him be tutored in my home."

Although the words came reluctantly, the instant joy that transformed her face made him want to repeat himself.

A sudden memory of Genna's eyes dampened the impulse. A little over a year ago she'd sat across from him. It was his fault she wasn't there tonight. *Remember.*

"Thank you, Michael. It'll be good for him to have a male role model—not that I expect you to spend time with him or anything—"

"Don't push," he said gruffly. "And he's welcome only so long as he behaves. One wrong step and he's out on his ear."

She didn't appear intimidated in the least. Her eyes merry, she asked, "What changed your mind?"

"For one thing, seeing him do his best to cheer

Jamie up this afternoon. When he tried to stand on his head…''

"With his feet flailing the air like he was riding a bike," Brynn added, laughing.

"And those faces he made…"

"I know! You'd think he was taking the SAT, he looked so intent. And when she hardly seemed to notice him, it was, 'Look at me, Jamie, look at me!' as though he'd accomplished a miracle."

"Maybe he had. He didn't look too experienced in headstanding."

"I think not," she said, her smile fond as she sipped her chocolate.

He thought about stopping there but found he couldn't.

"The other reason was you."

"Me?"

"I figured if you were willing to invest so much time and such a great portion of your salary to help him, something must be there."

"Michael, I never said I donated the money for those dolls."

"And you never said you didn't." He turned his head to the side, probing. "You're the most truthful person I know. Are you going to deny it?"

She pressed her lips together and stared at the darkness waiting beyond the window.

"Thank you. That's all the answer I need."

"It doesn't matter where the money came from. The important thing is that these dolls get finished on time, so some of our tutoring spots may be converted to assembly-line work, I'm afraid. You don't have anything against child labor, do you?''

"Not so long as I get my cut," he said, trying to answer her levity in kind, but a wave of sorrow swept away his smile and made his words heavy and slow.

He couldn't imagine having such a conversation with Genna. She had been too fearful to expose Jamie to many children, especially one like Chad who might contaminate her with physical disease or expose her to language and practices not their own.

Had he been wrong in changing his mind about Chad? This was not what his wife would have wanted.

"Michael?"

He glanced up to see Brynn observing him thoughtfully, and sipped coffee to hide his reluctance to speak.

"Are you all right?" she asked.

"I'm fine," he answered shortly. Without meeting her eyes, he went to the coffeemaker and poured a fresh cup. When he returned to his seat, he pulled farther away from the table, turning his chair toward the kitchen rather than her.

"That's good, because sometimes—like now, for instance—I feel you're drifting a thousand miles away. You can be so funny, so interested in other people, and then suddenly you're just...gone."

He considered brushing her off with a flippant answer, but her concern was too genuine to treat her like a child. And given the tenor of his thoughts during the past hour, it wasn't such a bad idea to warn her off, because he'd be warning himself at the same time.

"Do you ever get lost in memories, Brynn?"

"Oh, yes."

"That's where I go, I guess." He draped a forearm on the table and fingered his coffee cup. "I'm sure by now you've heard about the accident that took my wife's life." When she nodded slowly, he went on, "We were returning from a chamber of commerce banquet a few days before Christmas a year ago. It was a beautiful night—crisp, clear and with a sky full of stars. We were brimming over with plans for Jamie's Christmas, both of us talking a hundred miles a minute. Maybe if it had been foggy or rainy I'd have been more cautious."

He shrugged.

"But I wasn't. I stopped at a traffic light, waited for the green, then looked both ways and pulled into the intersection signaling a left. While I sat waiting for a break in the oncoming traffic, a pickup ran the red light and plowed into Genna's side of the car. She was killed instantly. The other driver died five days later without regaining consciousness. He'd been drinking. Usually it's the drunk who walks away, but not this time. I was the one who hardly received a scratch."

She reached toward him. When she fell shy of taking his hand, he breathed relief.

"The accident was a tragedy, but it wasn't your fault," she said.

"Technically, no. But had I been more alert I

would've seen the other car coming and avoided him.''

"You're being too hard on yourself."

"Not nearly hard enough. I was careless and Genna paid the ultimate price."

"Do you think it would have been better if you'd died, too?'' She gestured earnestly. "Can you imagine what would've happened to Jamie if you had?''

"You don't understand, Brynn. This isn't just about survivor's guilt."

"Then *make* me understand."

He sighed. "I promised to take care of Genna. She gave up everything to marry me, even her family. When we met, her father was old money, and I was just a poor kid serving time in the military, far from home in the Pacific Northwest."

Brynn, elbows on table, propped her chin in her hands. "But you swept her off her feet."

"You've been watching too many old movies. Genna's father was James Wade. *His* father had built a shipping empire in Seattle, which James expanded considerably. He ran his family like he did his work.

"Genna was expected to marry her childhood sweetheart, who just happened to be the son of an old family friend and business partner. When I blundered on the scene, she was ready to rebel for the first and only time in her life. After James saw we were serious about each other, he threatened to cut her off without a penny. He thought that would stop us, but he was wrong."

"Good for you both!'' she declared.

Her enthusiasm shot him back to the tired bliss of those early days. It was the first time in a long while he'd recalled them with fondness.

"It wasn't so good at first. We married, I finished my military time, then went through school on the GI bill while both of us worked at minimum-wage jobs. We struggled because her father meant what he said. Not only did he stop her allowance, he never spoke to her again."

"What about her mother?" Brynn asked indignantly.

"She died when Genna was seventeen. There was a stepmother soon after, but the two of them never got along."

"Well, you certainly proved him wrong, making yourself a professional and financial success."

"I wanted to replace what she'd lost." The attractions of his brief foray into the past dissipated. "But had she stayed in Seattle, she'd still be alive."

"You don't know that. And even if she were, she probably would have been unhappy and always wondering why. I'm sure if given the choice she'd choose the same path again."

"But she wasn't given the choice. She was robbed, and so was Jamie."

She gave him a hopeless look and shook her head. The gesture filled him with conflicting emotions. He didn't need her sympathy, nor did he deserve it.

"I'd better get to work," he said. "You should try and sleep. You'll need the rest. Jamie's usually cranky the day after a nightmare."

"I'll try."

He headed toward his study, then paused at the door. Brynn had risen and was stretching her arms ceilingward in a silent yawn. Even in that unconscious pose she looked graceful, as lithe and fascinating to watch as a kitten. The thought saddened him.

"Brynn."

Down fell her arms. She swerved, flushed, then gave him a wide, shamed smile. "Oh, sorry. I guess I am sleepy after all."

"Good." He hesitated, not wishing to hurt her but knowing he had to go on. "I want you to consider something."

"Sure, anything."

She gazed at him with absolute trust, her crystal-blue eyes conveying her eagerness to help. He doubted anything could make him feel worse.

"You're only going to be here a few months, and I can't help noticing how Jamie seems to be growing attached to you. I'm worried that when you leave, she'll be hurt."

"Oh, but I plan to visit occasionally if it's all right with you," she said. "Maybe take her to a movie or out for ice cream. I feel very attached to her."

"That would be fine," he said stiffly, "but I think we could avoid some of the upset if you'd just back off a little now."

Her smile faded. "Back off?"

"Yes. You know what I mean. Don't be

so…indispensable. Keep her at arm's length so she won't get too close.''

''I don't think I can do that,'' she said in bewildered tones. ''I don't know how.''

That was what he was afraid of, but he'd had to give it a try. He nodded, gave her a distracted smile and retreated to his study. After flipping on the lamp, he sat at the drafting table and stared numbly at his dream project. His work suddenly seemed an exercise in futility, without real meaning, a fairy-tale place too idealistic for the real world. He ran his fingers through his hair in frustration, then softly drummed his fist on the edge of the table. No matter what he did, he couldn't get his mind off Brynn.

''Back off yourself,'' he whispered. ''Just…back off.''

Chapter Ten

The next few weeks passed too quickly for Brynn, who struggled to find time for all the things that needed to be done.

She'd always had a tendency to overcommit herself, but at this point she was grateful for her busyness. The frantic pace helped keep her equilibrium following Michael's cautions about Jamie, which she still didn't understand.

Could he possibly want her to be aloof toward his daughter instead of giving her the love she needed? She couldn't believe he'd prefer Jamie to suffer now in order to save her pain later. Life should be lived full speed ahead, shouldn't it? "I am come that they might have life, and that they might have it more abundantly...."

Brynn was thinking about it one afternoon in March as she, Jamie and Chad sat in the family room attaching green bands around tiny black hats.

"If you could go to the greatest amusement park in the world," she said, squinting as she cut another felt band and added it to the pile, "the kind of park that has all your favorite rides—"

"The merry-go-round?" quizzed Jamie.

"That's for babies," Chad said. "It's got to have a roller coaster."

"Sure, all of those and more. Let's say you had the greatest time ever, but on your way out of the park you sprain your ankle. Would it have been better to stay home and not gotten hurt, or would you say it was worth the pain to have had the fun day at the park?"

"Stay home," Jamie said firmly. "Then go another day when I wouldn't get hurt."

"I'd go and not sprain my ankle," Chad said. "Boys don't fall a lot like stupid girls do."

"Girls are not stupid!" Jamie declared.

Brynn stared at them. "Thanks. That was incredibly helpful."

"What is this, Philosophy 101?" Michael asked from the doorway.

She looked up uncomfortably. Since the night of Jamie's nightmare she'd felt awkward around her employer, and it wasn't only because of his strange request regarding Jamie.

The way he looked at her sometimes... She found it increasingly difficult to view him only as her boss.

Jamie squeezed between the coffee table and Chad to lift sticky fingers upward. "Hey, Daddy, I wasn't 'specting you till supper."

"Hi, precious. I finished early today." He gave her a hug, exchanged greetings with Brynn and Chad, and sat in the maroon leather recliner opposite the sofa. "So what's going on?"

Chad scowled. "Hats. Hats and more stupid hats."

Brynn looked at him with worry. His tone had been increasingly irritable lately, and she wondered if the battle with the Family and Children's Services Division was getting to him, as she believed it was getting to his grandmother. Caseworkers had begun the home study and were asking all sorts of questions. Certainly the pressure hadn't helped the elderly woman, who had felt unwell recently and had even fallen behind in her quota of dolls.

"Barring disaster, we should make the deadline for the PTA fund-raiser," she told Michael.

"Congratulations. The three of you make quite a team."

"Jamie and Chad are wonderful, and so are Barbara and the volunteers from the Loving Meals program. Without them helping Chad's grandmother, we wouldn't have had a chance to finish in time."

"Anything I can do to help?"

Trying to hide her surprise, Brynn said, "Do you prefer tacking or scissors?"

"Whatever you need most."

"You cut and I'll help the munchkins." She handed him scissors and the adhesive-backed felt, pointing to the grid she'd drawn on back as a pattern. "Okay, guys. The three of us are in a race against Michael."

"I don't think those odds are quite fair," he said.

"Yes, but look at the stack we have left, while you couldn't have more than twenty or so to cut."

"Twenty? Surely there's at least fifty here."

Jamie bounced her bottom on the edge of the sofa. "What will we win?"

"How about ice cream at Pete's after supper?" Michael answered. "Loser pays."

"Yeah!" Jamie cried.

"But the work has to be good," Brynn cautioned. "Sloppy tacking or cutting doesn't count."

They worked quietly for a while as Brynn struggled to keep her mind from speculating on Michael's sudden friendliness. She hadn't been able to be more distant with Jamie as he'd asked—truth was, she hadn't even tried—but *he'd* certainly absented himself from them.

Eventually she'd concluded he didn't want to be around *her*, so she'd taken to spending a couple of hours in her room after dinner, after she took Chad home. And sure enough, every time she retired to her elegant bedroom with a book or to watch the widescreen television hidden behind a priceless Louis XV cabinet, she would hear the sounds of father and daughter talking and laughing together drifting upward from the family room.

His actions made her feel excluded, but better that than he neglect his daughter. Yet here he was tonight. She would never understand him.

Suddenly Chad threw down the hat in his hands. "My fingers hurt."

Get 2

HOW TO GET YOUR
2 FREE BOOKS AND FREE GIFT

1. Peel off the 2 FREE BOOKS seal from the front cover. Place it in the space provided at right. This automatically entitles you to receive two free books and an exciting mystery gift.

2. Send back this card and you'll get 2 Love Inspired® novels. These books have a combined cover price of $9.00 in the U.S. and $10.50 in Canada, but they are yours to keep absolutely FREE!

3. There's <u>no</u> catch. You're under <u>no</u> obligation to buy anything. We charge nothing – ZERO – for your first shipment. And you don't have to make any minimum number of purchases – not even one!

4. We call this line Love Inspired because each month you'll receive novels that are filled with joy, faith and true Christian values. The stories will lift your spirits and gladden your heart! You'll like the convenience of getting them delivered to your home well before they are in stores. And you'll like our discount prices too!

5. We hope that after receiving your free books you'll want to remain a subscriber. But the choice is yours – to continue or cancel, anytime at all! So why not take us up on our invitation, with no risk of any kind. You'll be glad you did!

6. And remember…we'll send you a mystery gift ABSOLUTELY FREE just for giving Love Inspired   a try!

Steeple
Hill®

SPECIAL
FREE GIFT!

We'll send you a fabulous mystery gift, absolutely FREE, simply for accepting our no-risk offer!

Books FREE!

DETACH AND MAIL CARD TODAY!

HURRY! **Return this card promptly to get 2 FREE books and a FREE gift!**

Love Inspired®

YES, send me the 2 FREE *Love Inspired* novels and FREE gift, as explained on the back. I understand that I am under no obligation to purchase anything further.

Affix peel-off 2 FREE BOOKS sticker here.

NAME   (PLEASE PRINT CLEARLY)

ADDRESS

APT.#   CITY

STATE/PROV.   ZIP/POSTAL CODE

303 IDL CQEK   **103 IDL CQEL**

(LI-LA-01/00)

"Take a break, then," Michael said.

"Don't break," commanded Jamie. "Daddy will win!"

"I don't care about any old contest. I want to go home."

With a chill of foreboding, Brynn set down her supplies. "What's wrong, Chad?"

"Nothing, I just want to go home."

"Why? You'll miss the ice cream."

Lowering his head, he dug the tip of his gym shoe into the carpet. "I got stuff to do, that's all."

"I'm sorry, Chad, but your grandmother was going out. Surely she told you. The senior citizen center is having special music tonight, and she's not expecting you back until nine."

"I'm not a baby. I don't need nobody to watch me."

Michael placed the scissors and felt on the coffee table. "If you're not a baby, then stop acting like one. Grown-up men understand rules and follow them, even when they don't like it."

Brynn looked anxiously from him to Chad. If Michael had spoken to her in that tone of voice, she would have wilted like a blossom in the desert. But the boy only looked more sullen.

"Is something wrong at school?" she asked gently.

"No."

"Are you sure you and Mrs. Jewell aren't having more problems?"

"No more than ever. She's a pain."

"She's a pig-woman," Jamie said eagerly, sliding to her feet.

Michael gave both children a stern look. "Teachers work very hard and don't deserve the kind of words you're using. I don't want to hear either of you talk that way again."

Chad's lips turned downward. "Can I go to the playroom?"

"Can I, too?" Jamie asked. "I'm tired of this stuff."

"Of course you may," Brynn said. "If your father doesn't mind."

Michael waved them toward the door, and the children ran off. "Looks like we've been stuck with the stuff," he said, taking scissors in hand again.

"It does get tedious after a while." She answered absently, her attention focused on a piece of paper that had fallen from Chad's back pocket. She went to the doorway and picked it up, unfolded it. "They lasted longer than usual today, though…oh."

"What?"

She returned to the sofa, still scanning the note. "This letter is from school—"

"Has he been expelled?"

If she hadn't spotted a twinkle in his eye, Brynn might have taken offense. "No, he hasn't been expelled." She returned to the letter. "This is an invitation to a family picnic at school in April. It's an all-day physical fitness event, and moms and dads are encouraged to stay and participate as long as they can. Poor Chad. Poor all the kids without moms and dads. How can they do this to the children—don't they realize how many families are broken these days? Oh, wait. I take it back.''

She darted a glance at him, then fell silent.

The sounds of scissors cutting cloth continued a moment longer, then stopped.

''I hate suspense, Brynn.''

With a tentative smile, she said, ''I'm trying to decide whether or not to tell you what it says.''

''I gathered that,'' he said dryly.

''The note gives children permission to bring family members or representatives, such as Big Brothers or Sisters.''

They studied one another for a moment.

''We've been had,'' he said finally.

''I don't know about that, but I do think Chad's dropping the note was no accident. This is dated last week, which means he made a special point of carrying it. Poor kid. He knows his grandmother can't participate. I wonder if the thought of this picnic has been troubling him. But of course it has.''

She broke from her reverie. ''I think I'd better go to the event. I'll take Jamie, too, if you don't mind.''

His hesitation was so slight as to be almost non-existent. ''I'm sure it'll be good for her to get acquainted with the school environment. If work permits, I might try to put in an appearance, too.''

''How wonderful,'' she said, too amazed to generate the enthusiasm she knew she should feel.

''I can see you don't believe me, but I do intend

to try. I've made a decision to spend more time with Jamie, even if Chad's there, too.''

His phrasing broke her heart. "Is Chad so bad?"

"Not really, except that he reminds me of myself at that age. I do have to say things were easier without him, but Jamie likes the boy and doesn't seem any the worse for wear. In fact, she's acting brighter these days. I have to give him credit for part of that.''

A glow spread across her body. He couldn't have said anything that would have made her happier.

"I'm glad you're going to try to be with Jamie more often.''

"You should be. It's your fault.''

"Mine?''

"Yes. When Jamie and I are together without you, it's *Brynn says this* and *Brynn does that*. In the hope of becoming a major character in her life, I'm taking a page from your book. I want to get her involved with more people, more interests that we both can share. She's become so dependent on you it's the only way I know to reduce the pain of separation when you go.''

She could hardly contain her smile. He might not realize it, but his willingness to engage Jamie in more activities meant that *he* was reaching outward, too. The terrible blow of his wife's death might not be fatal for him after all.

"If it's any comfort to you, when Jamie's with me, it's *Daddy says this* and *Daddy would let me do that*.''

He grinned. "The girl is playing us like a pair of fiddles."

"She's a real prodigy," Brynn said with a giggle.

"You only have to look at the two of us to see it. Snip snip, cut cut."

"Paste paste. We've only got a week to finish."

"Spring fling, here we come," he said, and took up the scissors once more.

It was a dangerous path he trod, Michael thought on the following Thursday evening as he helped Brynn monitor the doll booth at Sherwin Falls Elementary School's Annual Spring Fair.

Being around Brynn made him uneasy. She forced him to laugh more than he should. With her optimism and even nature, she reminded him of the good things he'd once felt before the world went wrong: hope, trust, faith. With a longing that tasted bittersweet, he wished he could feel that way again.

But it was impossible. He didn't deserve happiness, and he couldn't reclaim his faith. That Genna had died needlessly proved to him events occurred at random. There was no guiding hand leading God's children through life, therefore God did not exist. If He did, where was He when Genna needed Him?

He would rather die a doubter than to believe in a God who allowed tragedies to happen.

Michael's presence at this raucous festival was only because Brynn had driven him to it. She wouldn't step back from Jamie, so he had to step forward. His child needed him.

Oh, who did he think he was fooling? he asked himself as he handed change to a young mother buying a leprechaun for her toddler. *I should have listened to my first instincts and never hired her.*

Spending time with Brynn was as invigorating as standing beneath a waterfall on a hot day.

He enjoyed her company, plain and simple. Nothing more than that. There was no reason to fear his feelings ran deeper.

"We've sold forty-seven already," Brynn whispered to him as a customer walked away. "And we've still got two hours to go!"

"Boy, oh boy," he said. Two more hours.

A lifetime.

"Daddy, I want to see the other zibits," Jamie whined from her stool inside the ten-by-ten structure confining the three of them. Earlier she had played store by stacking the dolls on shelves. Now she wouldn't touch the leprechauns, and Michael couldn't blame her. "You let Chad go."

"Why don't you take her around," Brynn urged. "I can manage."

Relieved, he took Jamie's hand and pulled her through the stall gate and to the maze of booths and games set up on the school's parking lot. With a good crowd of families and patches of young teens wandering around, the fair looked to be a success.

Several cooks were grilling chicken, hamburgers and hot dogs, and the smells made him ravenous. He bought a hot dog for his daughter and himself. He hoped Chad had spent at least some of the money he'd given him tonight on food. Before Jamie would eat, he had to promise to buy one for Brynn later.

As they strolled from one booth to the next, Michael found himself growing sentimental. The scene reminded him of something he couldn't remember, some similar event from his childhood, perhaps, or maybe a fragment of a dream. It made him nostalgic for a better world, a simpler time.

But maybe life didn't get finer than this. With Jamie's hand tucked in his, he felt as if he could solve any problem, conquer any adversary.

As night drew closer, however, his mood darkened.

What lies he told himself. He couldn't save anyone. In the heedless flow of life, he was as helpless as a twig in a raging flood.

He was lost.

Just like everyone else.

"Daddy, can I have one of those?"

His attention returned to Jamie, who was tugging at his hand while pointing to a stack of friendship bracelets. He bought her one and attached it to her arm.

They had reached the end of the circuit. As he headed Jamie back the other way, he caught sight of a cluster of children near the school, one of them very familiar.

On second look, he saw that Chad was the only child in the foursome, while the other boys must have been in their early teens. Two of them were dragging on cigarettes, their furtive looks at the parking lot indicating how nervous their own daring made them.

Michael stiffened with disapproval. This was the kind of thing Genna would have frowned on—Chad's association with the wrong element. It was inevitable he'd bring what he learned to their daughter.

"Let's go, Daddy," Jamie said, unable to understand why her father stood so motionlessly staring into the dark.

"Just a second, baby."

Something was wrong with that group of boys. Other than the obvious, of course. From Chad's body language, Michael realized that he didn't like the attention of the big guys. In fact, he appeared threatened by them.

But he wasn't going to back down. When one of the teens stepped into his personal space, Chad refused to shrink back and eyed his opponent with every sign of defiance.

Good for you, Michael thought, and wondered at the astonishing surge of pride he felt.

Still, another minute or two and the child could very well be ground to a pulp. Michael asked the lady in the bracelet booth, an acquaintance of his and Genna's, to watch Jamie for a minute. After lifting his protesting daughter into the stall, he strode across the grass toward the building.

Funny how fast those cigarettes disappeared when the boys noticed him. Only then did Chad sense his approach and turn. Surprisingly, he failed to look as cheered by his rescue as Michael expected.

Nevertheless, Michael greeted the group as politely as he would a potential client.

"Chad, are you about ready to join us at the booth?" he inquired easily.

"Who's he?" asked the tallest boy, a skinny fellow just beginning to spot.

Chad gave Michael a strange glance, as if he didn't know what to call him. Finally he said, "That's Mr. Hudson."

"I'm Chad's Big Brother," Michael said, letting his gaze roam from one face to the next. "Is there a problem here?"

"Nah," said Tall Boy. "C'mon, let's go." He jutted his chin toward the back of the school, then added to Chad, "Talk to you later, *little brother*." He laughed insolently, his adolescent giggles sending shivers of distaste down Michael's spine. Hopefully he had never sounded like that.

The boys slunk away, leaving Michael and Chad alone. Michael nodded toward the parking lot, and they began the return walk.

"What was that all about?"

"Nothing. Just some guys I know."

"Looked to me like they were up to no good."

"We was just talking."

Try as he would, Michael could get no more out of him.

But for the rest of the evening, he made sure Chad

stayed near their stall. Even though Chad wasn't his responsibility.

Maybe it wasn't such a bad idea for Human Resources to step in after all. Even though it would pain Brynn, Chad and his grandmother, he believed it was for the best. That sweet old lady couldn't keep up with a child like him. Blindness aside, she was in no condition to keep him close enough to monitor. And monitoring—strong parental guidance—was what Chad needed more than anything.

The boy was showing all the signs of a kid headed for trouble: his temper, his moodiness, his dislike of authority. As the evening wore on, Michael watched him covertly, losing track of him only when Brynn jumped over the cubicle to hawk her five remaining dolls with a comical, dramatic sales pitch that drew a small crowd. The potential customers could no more resist her than he could. His final contribution of the night was the purchase of the last two dolls, which he promised to award to his office staff for good behavior.

That was when he noticed Chad had gone missing again, and while Brynn and Jamie closed shop, he hurried from one booth to the next, all the time dreading he'd find him back in the shadows.

But he found Chad at the cake walk, and even when the boy won a three-layer coconut cake on his first try, he gave merely a halfhearted smile as he scanned the crowd, looking, looking. Who did he expect to see?

This was not the child he'd come to know during

the past couple of months, and Michael felt a shock of concern for him. Chad might be headed for delinquency, but there was something else behind his blue-circled eyes and pale face.

Fear.

she had enough of coffee, but Kirstof fell victim of it again for his. Chauncoln or Jackel in Dick quotes, but there are such and one behind it Blacmetic overnight his face

Chapter Eleven

"You're getting all dressed up," Jamie said in accusing tones.

Brynn stopped powdering her cheeks to meet the child's eyes in the makeup mirror. "Yes, I have an interview this morning. Remember, I told you about it yesterday?"

"*Another* one?"

Setting down the powder puff, she turned to the child. She was seated at the vanity table in their shared bathroom, and Jamie was leaning her forearms on the sink countertop.

"It's only my third interview. You know I have to get another job eventually. Nanny Sue will be coming back in a few months."

The words pained her like a sore throat. She didn't like thinking about the end of the summer any more than Jamie did, but she'd diligently begun to mention it periodically. It was the closest she could come to distancing herself as Michael had asked.

How could it be the last week of April already?

"Nanny Sue might have to stay with her mommy longer."

"That would mean her mother would still be sick, and I'm sure you want her to get well."

The child appeared to think about it. "Why can't you both be my nannies?"

Brynn signaled for her to come closer, then took her hands. "It doesn't work that way, honey. Just remember that I'll come to see you often."

Jamie wriggled free and flounced into her bedroom.

You have an amazing way with children, she told her reflection sadly.

Descending the stairs a few minutes later, she found Barbara dusting the living-room furniture and told her she was leaving. As she passed through the hall, the door to the study opened.

"Off to your interview?" Michael asked.

For an instant she could think of nothing to say. He was wearing khakis and a blue sweater that warmed the color of his eyes and quickened her heartbeat. Amazing how attractive he was. Sometimes she found it hard to speak to him, and the problem seemed to be growing worse.

"Um, yes. I'm a little nervous about this one."

"Because it's at Chad's school."

"Right. I interviewed with the principal when I first moved here, but it wasn't in-depth like it will be today, since he knows about definite openings now. I'd really like to get a position there.''

''You'll do fine. I hear principals like teacher involvement, and Mr. Bridges appeared friendly when he came by your leprechaun booth at the fair. It probably wouldn't be a bad idea to make a point of seeing him Friday at Family Day, too.''

''I'll try to do that. Mr. Bridges seems nice, but I have a feeling he's hard to please.''

She recalled her words as she sat in the principal's office a half hour later. Nervously she glanced at the sparse furniture and paneled walls, which were decorated with framed degrees and photographs of Bridges posed beside local dignitaries—the fire chief, the sheriff and a man she recognized as the mayor. Although she'd been in this office on two occasions, once for her initial interview and another for Chad, she noticed for the first time that each frame was black with a slender gold stripe, and the rows were aligned with military precision.

Mr. Bridges was just as exacting in his questions. He maintained a professional distance throughout the interview until his final query.

''Suppose you have a problem child in your classroom. He hits the other children and talks back to you. How will you handle it?''

This was the kind of question for which she'd been prepared in her training. She spoke of various classroom management techniques, knowing the important thing was to resort to the principal last. Although strong leadership was one of the hallmarks of a successful school, most principals didn't want to be bothered with petty discipline problems. Mr. Bridges would expect her to try to manage the dilemma herself if she could.

Evidently her answer pleased him, for he gave her a warm handshake and promised to let her know before school was out in June.

She paused at the door, desperate to ask how Chad was doing but knowing she shouldn't. She had no legal right to seek information about the boy, and she couldn't beg the principal to breach ethics. And then he brought up the subject himself.

"You've done a really good job with Chad Boyd," he said. "Mrs. Jewell tells me his grades are up."

"I'm so glad. He's a sweet child."

Mr. Bridges chuckled. "I'll take your word for it."

"Why, has he been in trouble again?" In the evenings the boy continued to act strangely, often surly and tense, and problems at school might be part of the explanation.

"No, matter of fact, he's acted very quiet lately. Must be your good influence."

She thanked him and pretended to smile. Walking through the halls and to the van, she wished she could fool herself into thinking Chad's quiet signaled improvement, but she suspected it was only the silence before the storm.

Family Day at Sherwin Falls Elementary dawned cloudy, but by nine, the time activities were scheduled to begin, the sun had burned its way through and the day promised to be fair. Michael lugged folding chairs to the school playground while Brynn and Jamie hurried along beside him. Although she regretted that Chad's grandmother hadn't been well enough to accompany them, Brynn felt as excited as a child. When Jamie began to skip, she did, too, both of them holding hands and laughing.

"Here we go, kiddies," Michael said tolerantly, unfolding the chairs beneath the shade of a newly leafed elm. "But I guess you youngsters have too much energy to sit."

"I'll sit," Jamie said, and did so, delicately. After two seconds she shot up again. "All done sitting!" she giggled.

"Why, you little..." Michael growled, and seized her high in his arms. The child's delighted laughter rang out, drawing the eyes of other parents standing nearby, some of them responding with amused looks.

Brynn wistfully bit her lip through her smile. To strangers they must seem like a family. A very happy family.

Lines of children began to pour from the school building, and Jamie demanded that Michael hold her aloft so that Chad would see them. He did so groaningly, and before long the boy was trotting toward them.

"Where's lunch?" he said by way of greeting. He looked more like his old self, Brynn was pleased to see. His eyes gleamed as if he were determined to enjoy this novel day outside the classroom.

Michael laughed at him. "Lunch? It's not even nine-thirty."

"Yeah, but where is it?"

Brynn realized he was afraid they'd forgotten. "We left the food in the van in the cooler. We have all kinds of sandwiches and fruit and cold drinks, so there'll be plenty."

The public address system squealed into action, and Mr. Bridges announced the first field event, the egg-and-spoon tag race. Teams were divided by grade level, and each child was to be partnered by an adult.

When Michael and Chad went off together, Jamie immediately became restless. Suddenly inspired, Brynn grabbed the child's hand and went in search of the kindergarten line. Begging the friendliest-looking teacher she could find—Ms. Turner, a striking brunette who appeared to be Brynn's age—she received permission for Jamie and herself to take part in the games so long as they didn't expect a prize if they won.

Out of four kindergarten classrooms, Jamie's team came in second. Chad's classroom placed third among five second grades. Ribbons were awarded to first- and second-place winners. Jamie stood disconsolately watching as the prizes were handed out, until Ms. Turner suddenly gave her one.

"I think we'll have enough for her to receive this," she told a protesting Brynn.

Thanking her, Brynn added impulsively, "I've applied for a teaching job here next year."

"Did you? Well, good luck. It's not a perfect school, but we have a lot of advantages—good faculty relationships and dedication to technology...."

They talked a few minutes longer before the next race. By lunchtime, Brynn felt as if she'd made a new friend. Now she had another reason for hoping Mr. Bridges would decide in her favor.

Since she'd be unable to keep her favorite job, she had to find ways to build enthusiasm for what came next. She must begin to plan for a future without Jamie.

And without Michael, breathed a small voice, which she wished away.

When she and Jamie arrived back at their chairs, Michael and Chad had already fetched the cooler and were spreading a blanket beneath the elm. The next few moments passed in agreeable chatter as Brynn distributed food on paper plates.

Halfway through the meal, she realized Chad had fallen into one of his silences again. She thought of trying to draw him out, but she'd done that multiple times to no avail. For one so young, he had an amazing ability to keep his troubles to himself. Perhaps he didn't know how to articulate them.

Maybe she could help.

"If you had one wish that would be granted, what would you wish for?" she asked them.

"World peace," Michael said quickly.

She made a face at his lack of originality. "What about you, Jamie?" she asked, then cringed. Naturally the child would wish for her mother back, and the rest of the day would be spoiled. So much for child psychology.

"I'd wish you could be my nanny for always."

Tears bubbling to her eyes, Brynn hugged her. "Thank you, sweetie." She sniffed, then turned to Chad. "And what would you want?"

For an instant she thought he wouldn't answer, but then he said, "That God wouldn't be mad at me."

She exchanged a shocked look with Michael. "What makes you think God is mad at you?"

"Nothing. He just might be." The boy's lids fell. "That's all."

"Is that what they've been teaching you at church?" Michael said on a forbidding note, his gaze pinning Brynn.

She shriveled inside. Did he think this was her fault?

The boy said, "God hates sinners and punishes them."

"Oh, Chad," Brynn moaned. "He doesn't hate sinners, but He does despise sin, because it separates us from His love."

"Sin is wrong," Jamie pronounced, and then added in an interested voice, "You been sinning?"

"Would you listen to these children?" Michael said, looking at Brynn in outrage.

"Wait," she begged him. "Chad, would you take a walk with me?"

When he shrugged, she led him to a far corner of the playground, where she urged him to sit beside her in the grass.

"Something's troubling you," she began, "and I don't really think you're worried about the Lord's anger, are you?"

"One of the boys in Sunday school class said God makes bad people die."

"Well, you've been listening to the wrong person." She stared across the field, remembering similar fears from her own childhood. What was it her mother had said to her?

"We all do bad things, Chad. When that happens we should pray and ask God's forgiveness. If we really mean that we're sorry, if we try very hard not to do that wrong thing again, He'll forgive us. God wants us to talk with Him because He loves us so very much. Do you understand?"

"I guess."

She studied his face. "Is there something you want to pray about right now?"

"No!" He gave her a sideways look, then said in calmer tones, "I mean, I'll do it tonight at home."

"Good. You don't have to tell me what's bothering you if you don't want. Just be sure you talk it over with your heavenly Father, okay?"

"I will."

"Great!" She struggled to put enthusiasm into her voice, for Chad's fears hurt her deeply. Giving him a swift hug, she said, "I love you, guy. Ready to go back?"

"Yeah."

Michael's gaze switched back and forth between them when they returned. As Chad began to act more normally, he seemed to relax. The conversation over dessert was only slightly strained.

Before long, the principal returned to his microphone to announce the afternoon games. Jamie had grown tired, and while Michael and Chad participated in various competitions, Brynn cheered them on as the child slept on the blanket.

She couldn't fail to note how well Michael interacted with Chad. He led the child with a firmer hand than she would have, but the boy responded to him. More than once she caught a flash of hero worship in Chad's eyes when he glanced at Michael. And no wonder. She'd be surprised if her own expression didn't reflect the same.

Even with his problems of grief and guilt, he was exemplary. His tenderness toward Jamie and his kindness to Chad made him outstanding in her eyes. And though he might wrestle with spiritual issues, Michael Hudson was a good man.

Her gaze returned to him again and again as the afternoon wore on.

And then, during the last event of the day as she watched him and Chad struggle valiantly toward the finish line to place second in the sack race, she felt something within her crack. When Michael lifted the boy to his shoulders, both of them grinning ear-to-ear as they held high their ribbons, the crack widened to a fissure, and light poured into her heart where a clot of bitterness had long been hidden, starving her soul for air.

Thank you, God, for preventing me from marrying the wrong man.

She had never loved Reed Blake. She'd *thought* she was in love, but her experience had been too limited. Reed's attraction had been in appearing to be the kind of man she believed her mother would have been proud to call son-in-law.

Now she understood the many levels of complexity that underlaid the real thing.

Love saw the flaws, but loved anyway. There might be no hope of reciprocation, yet love went on quietly and sometimes unspoken, always putting the welfare of the loved one first.

She understood this was love, pure and selfless, because in one blinding flash she knew she loved Michael Hudson.

She'd done exactly what she promised not to do during her first interview with him.

How convincingly she had assured him she never wanted to get married. She'd meant it then. At that time she was certain she couldn't love again, because Reed had hurt her too badly.

In spite of a slight physical resemblance, Michael wasn't like Reed, and she was wrong to have lied to herself because of it. Michael had flaws like everyone else, but he was a different sort of man altogether. His enduring love for his late wife proved it.

Nothing would come of her feelings, of course. Even if Michael could learn to love her and conquer his guilt and sorrow about his wife, too many problems stood between them. His rocky relationship with Chad, for one. The boy was becoming increasingly important to her, and she sensed Michael tolerated him only for Jamie's sake.

And the very worst barrier was his hostility toward her faith, which she had seen demonstrated only hours ago. How quickly he had turned accusing eyes on her when Chad and Jamie talked about God's wrath.

She had seen too many marriages torn apart by differing views on God. Even more damaging was what it did to the children. Parental battles over religion could destroy a child's faith, and she would never be a part of hurting Jamie.

Though there was no chance for them, she thanked God for stopping her from making the worst mistake of her life. Unimaginable to think what existence would have been like with Reed.

And to have never known love…that would have been worse than anything.

She looked up as the conquerors made a noisy return to the elm tree, proudly displaying a collection of ribbons and bringing Jamie to complaining wakefulness. Brynn comforted her while Michael put away the picnic paraphernalia and Chad rejoined his class to return inside the school.

When she failed to respond with her usual enthusiasm to Michael's conversational gambits, he eyed her curiously. "Hey, you never said what your wish would be if you were granted one."

"World peace," she answered immediately, and could not take her eyes off him as he laughed.

Chapter Twelve

What had he done wrong? Michael wondered. Several weeks had elapsed since the Family Day event, and Brynn hadn't been the same.

Greeting Barbara as she chopped onions and celery at the island, he went to the mail basket on the desk, saw several bills, tossed them back, then spotted a letter from Sue Baxter. He leaned against the countertop and tapped the envelope at his cheek, thinking only of Brynn.

Yes, it had been around that time she'd become distant. She continued to mind Jamie with warmth, she often brought Chad into their home, but toward him there was something different. She remained polite, but gone was the easy banter and the lightning smiles.

He didn't like the change. He didn't like it at all.

"Where's Brynn and Jamie?" he asked Barbara. "I saw the van was gone."

"I sent them to the store for a half gallon of ice cream. Strawberries are in and we're having short-cake for dessert."

"That's the best news I've heard all day."

He slit open the envelope and read as he walked into his study. A few minutes later the front doorbell rang. Dimly he thought of sparing Barbara the bother of answering it, but he couldn't move. Not yet. Too much to think about.

Gradually the voices in the hall filtered into his mind, and he laid Sue's letter on his desk and hurried to the door.

"Andy," he said heartily, his curious gaze skipping Barbara and moving to Brynn, then Jamie.

"We had a flat tire," Jamie said.

Brynn nodded. "I started to change it, but Andy came along and offered us a ride."

Michael sent his friend a polite smile. "*Did* he?"

"Yeah, the knight in shining armor, that's me," Andy said.

Brynn added, "We couldn't refuse his generosity, because the ice cream might have melted." She seemed unusually perky this afternoon, even for her.

"That would've been unthinkable," Michael agreed in a neutral tone of voice, noticing how Brynn's eyes glittered when she looked at Stetter.

His employee quickly added, "I've brought the revised plans for the Zinmeyer place. Thought you might want to look at them this weekend."

"Are you going to join us for dinner, Andy?" Barbara asked. "It's been months since the last time."

"Well...if you twisted my arm I might."

I'll twist your arm, Michael wanted to say, but he welcomed him in kind host fashion, taking the plans from his hand and inviting him to sit in the living room. Then he excused himself to call his auto club to rescue the van.

Dinner that evening passed more slowly than any meal in his memory. Stetter was in top form recounting stories of his army days—the only action he'd seen was shooting bazookas at tanks at Fort Benning—charm dripping like honey off his mustache every time he addressed one of the women. And the woman he addressed most was Brynn.

To give her credit, she didn't seem overwhelmed by the attention, but her responses flowed more easily toward Andy than himself, reminding him of the times when she giggled at *his* jokes and threw back remarks that made him laugh.

By the time the dessert plates were cleared away, he was in a foul mood. Stetter asked to see him in his study before he left, and Michael ushered him in with the last threads of his patience.

Andy unrolled the blueprints and pointed out the changes he'd made.

"Looks fine to me if the Zinmeyers are happy," Michael said, moving toward the door in the hopes Andy would take the hint. "I'll take a closer look tomorrow."

"There's one other thing I want to ask," Stetter said awkwardly. "Is anything going on between you and Jamie's nanny?"

"Don't be ridiculous!"

Andy grinned. "Good. Then you won't mind if I ask her out."

Michael felt a surge of anger and fought to control it.

"Yes, I do mind. Brynn's a young woman in my employ, and I feel responsible for her. And you have to admit you're not known for treating women well."

Stetter's smile had gradually faded during this response, and now his chin hardened. "I can see she's different, Michael. That's why I want to go out with her. Life after divorce isn't all it's cracked up to be. I'm getting tired of the singles scene. Brynn's gorgeous, but she's a sweetheart, too, the kind of woman a guy might want to settle down with if things work out. Don't worry, I'll handle her with kid gloves."

"You're not going to handle her with kid gloves or anything else, not while she works for me."

"Hey, Mike. Flash news—it's a free country." Andy's eyes glimmered. "Who do you think you are, her guardian?"

"No, I don't think I'm her guardian, but while she's in this house she's under my protection and I intend to watch out for her best interests."

Andy's face gradually relaxed. With a glint of amusement that infuriated Michael, he said, "Oh, okay, I see what's going on. Sorry, buddy, but you should have said something instead of pretending like she meant nothing to you."

"But she doesn't," Michael said. "Not in the way you're talking about."

Andy laughed and went to the door. "Sure, sure."

"Hey, wait—"

"Not me. I've got better things to do."

"Andy!"

But the door had closed.

Idiot. Thought he knew everything, when he could hardly tie his own shoelaces.

Michael simmered at his desk for a while, distracting himself by reading and rereading Sue's letter until he'd memorized it, debating the pros and cons of discussing this new development with Brynn.

But he was only delaying the inevitable. There was no question he wouldn't bring it up with her.

He flung open the door. "Brynn!" he yelled.

"Good heavens, Michael," said Barbara from the living room where she sat reading. "You'll give me a heart attack."

He apologized. Brynn appeared an instant later at the head of the stairs, and he asked her to come to his study for a moment.

"I'm glad you invited me here," Brynn said as she took a seat in front of his desk seconds later. He joined her in the companion chair, not wanting to sit with the desk between them. "I have some news to share that I've been dying to tell you all evening, but I didn't feel I should bring it up in front of a stranger."

Good. She thought of Andy as a stranger, and that was fine with him. "I have some news as well, but you go first."

"I got the job!"

"You did?" His voice sounded faint and thin to his ears, as if it came from a distant planet.

"Yes, at Sherwin Falls! I'm so happy."

He flinched a smile. "I imagine you are. Well, well. Congratulations."

"It's a third-grade classroom, my first choice. Maybe Chad will be in my room next year! Although on second thought that probably wouldn't be for the best. I'll have to ask the other teachers what they think."

She shook off her stream-of-consciousness. "Anyway, I thought I should tell you first, and I don't really want to mention it to Jamie until later unless you think I should."

"Hmm? Oh. No, you're right. It could ruin her summer."

She hesitated. "Surely it's not so severe as that. She knows I've applied for a teaching job."

"Yes, but applying and actually having one are two different things."

A worry line creased her brow. "You're probably right, but I'll have to tell her long before Nanny Sue comes back, because I'll be spending a lot of time preparing at school this summer."

Michael cleared his throat. "Nanny Sue's not coming back."

"What?"

"That's the news I was going to tell you. Her mother has asked her to live with her permanently. Sue feels like she should, because her mom needs round-the-clock help."

"Oh, I'm sorry to hear that." Her eyes widened. "Oh, no. That means you'll have to hire *another* nanny."

He studied her features for a moment, working up courage.

"Not necessarily," he said. "Not if you decided to stay on."

"Oh." Her face underwent a series of emotions. "This is such a surprise. There's nothing I'd like better than to stay with Jamie, but..." She closed her eyes briefly, and he wondered if she was praying. "I've already accepted the position."

"Have you signed a contract yet?"

"No, but I've given my word," she whispered, her gaze locking with his.

"Bridges will understand the change in circumstances. You can't tell me there aren't at least twenty other applicants hoping for that position."

"I'm sure you're right, but..."

"It happens all the time, Brynn."

She stood up suddenly and turned her back to him. "I'm sorry, I...just don't think it's a good idea."

"Why not? You said there was nothing you'd like more than to stay with Jamie."

When she didn't respond, he circled around to see her face. To his shock, tears were spilling down her cheeks.

"Brynn," he said, his voice inflecting with concern. Quickly he handed her his handkerchief, then stroked her upper arm until she flinched from his touch. "I'm sorry, I didn't mean to upset you."

She shook her head and gave a tearful smile. "You didn't. It's just hard when you have two things you want desperately and you have to choose between them. I love Jamie like my own life, but my dream has always been to teach school."

"You won't find a child in Sherwin Falls who needs you more than my daughter," he said.

"But I don't know if I'm *good* for her."

"You must be kidding. She hasn't had a nightmare in months. Dr. Coffield only wants to see her every six weeks now. No one has been better for her than you."

Not even her own mother, he almost said, but stopped short of the shocking words and wondered in disgust just how disloyal he could be.

When she looked down, his stomach clenched at the pain he saw in her expression. He had to stop badgering her. He was being too intense, too eager to get his own way.

"You don't understand," she said. "I'm afraid Jamie and I are becoming too close."

"Oh." He walked to his desk, unthinkingly sitting in his executive chair. "I see. You want to get on with your own life, and I can understand that would be hard when living in someone else's house."

"No, it's not that—"

"You're a young woman, and in spite of what you've experienced with that bum you almost married, you'll recover. Pretty soon you'll want to start dating again, and before you know it, you'll get married and have children of your own."

She gave him the strangest look, a round-eyed stare wavering between laughter and tears. "Sounds like you have my life all planned out for me."

"Well, you *should* have children, because you'd make a great mother."

"Thanks, but I'm not marrying anyone."

"A pretty woman like you? Don't make me laugh."

"My track record for attracting the kind of love that lasts is zero."

"Brynn," he said painfully, "you make it sound like that messed-up wedding was your fault. Don't take the blame for the actions of a heel, and don't let him shake your self-confidence. What he did was unconscionable. He was an idiot not to cherish a prize like you."

Her lashes fell. Certain she remained unconvinced, he gritted his teeth and said, "Why, only this evening Andy was talking about you."

She looked surprised, and he hoped she wasn't overly gratified. He'd only wanted to cheer her up, not put ideas in her head.

"Not that I'd recommend him as good dating material," he said firmly. "Andy's a great guy, but he has a reputation for stomping on female hearts."

"I sensed that."

"You did?" The wind died in his sails. "Well, good."

"I'm not naive, Michael. It's just…" Still standing, she leaned her arms on the back of the chair. "Some marriages seem to be made in heaven. Both husband and wife love each other intensely, and their hearts and minds are one—on the important issues, at least. Together, the man and woman are much more than they ever would have been apart. I don't want anything less than that.''

"You," he said, wagging his forefinger, "are a romantic."

"But that's the kind of marriage you had."

Her words startled him into a brief silence. "In many ways, yes, but no marriage is perfect."

"I'm sorry, I shouldn't have said anything," she replied, flushing. "I know how painful the loss of your wife has been, and to remind you was unforgivable."

"Genna is never far from my thoughts anyway, Brynn," he said truthfully.

"I know she isn't. That's the kind of love I mean, and I've seen how rarely it happens. So maybe you can understand why I don't plan on getting married. But I can have a full and happy life loving other people's children. After my mother died and I lived with a lot of different families, it was the children's love in those homes that sustained me."

There was a deep and painful history behind her words, Michael realized, and he felt slammed by sudden empathy. How had she survived with her tender spirit intact?

But she hadn't, not entirely. At the center of her heart, a hurting little girl lay hidden. A girl who believed she wasn't worthy of love.

"Oh, Brynn," he said, aching for her. "Someday you'll have the kind of love you're looking for."

"Please, Michael. Just…stop." She turned and walked to the door.

"Don't go without saying you'll at least *think* about staying on as Jamie's nanny," he blurted out.

Without looking at him, she said in a voice so quiet he had to strain to hear, "I'll think about it."

Over the next few days Brynn thought of little else but Michael's offer, and it became the focal concern of her prayers. There was no chance she could accept the extended position, of course. Now that her feelings for him were clear, even her love for Jamie couldn't make her consider living in the same house with a man she loved hopelessly.

Instead, she began to think about leaving earlier than the end of summer.

Michael had cautioned her to avoid getting too close to his daughter. It was already too late for that. Every day that passed, every activity the girl and she shared, cemented their bond further.

The only way she knew to stop the process was to leave. It would be hard, *wrenching,* for both of them now. In three more months the separation would be unbearable.

On the last Saturday before school was out for the summer, she was struggling to find the strength to talk with Michael when he brought up the subject himself.

The gardener had opened the pool, and Jamie's

friend from church, Candy Hayes, had arrived that afternoon for supper and a sleepover. While Michael grilled hot dogs, Brynn, from a poolside chair, watched the children swim.

When he settled into the chair next to her, Brynn started to rise. "Finished already? I'd better get the salad and chips."

He waved her back to her seat. "The food will keep. The kids are having too much fun to interrupt them."

She watched the girls as they piggybacked down the water slide, both of them squealing in delighted fear. This is how it should be for Jamie, she thought. The friendship with Chad is wonderful, but every child needs the companionship of his or her own gender.

Feeling Michael's eyes on her, Brynn looked at him questioningly.

"Have you given any more thought to what we were talking about the other day?" he asked.

Her mouth going dry, she turned her gaze back to the children. "Yes, I have."

He waited, then prompted impatiently, "And?"

"I believe it's for the best if I go on with my original plan."

"I see." He was quiet so long that her heart began to pound. "I have to say I'm disappointed."

"It was a difficult decision," she said awkwardly. "But I think it'll be better for Jamie."

"Do you?" He sounded skeptical, almost angry.

"I remember your advising me not to get too close—"

"But that was because you were an interim nanny. If you're her *permanent* one, that's different."

"But Michael, there would be some point when I'd have to leave!"

He met her eyes in surprise, as if this thought had never occurred to him.

"I keep forgetting how young you are," he admitted.

"Well, that's a surprise. You're the one who usually reminds *me*."

He smiled faintly. "And you have your whole life before you."

"Please don't start that again." How blind could he be? Didn't the man realize that being near him was sweet torture? "I've also been thinking that, since Sue isn't returning and you have to hire a new nanny anyway, maybe you should begin looking as soon as possible."

As the seconds dragged by, she could feel his eyes burning into her skin. She was afraid to look at him.

"Every day with Jamie is painful," she said finally. "The longer I stay, the harder it will be to part. If you find my replacement soon, Jamie and I could taper off our relationship. I'd have time during the summer to visit her almost every day at first, then gradually lengthen the interval between visits."

"You've got it all figured out, haven't you?"

She decided to ignore the note of bitterness she heard. "I've been talking with Marla Turner, one of the teachers at Sherwin Falls Elementary. She owns a house in town and rents out her basement apartment. At the end of June her current renter is leaving, and she's offered me the lease."

Michael stood abruptly. "You're going to destroy Jamie," he said.

She bounced from the chair and faced him with sudden, trembling anger. "How can you say such a thing? I'm trying to help her!"

"Daddy, what's wrong?"

Both of them swerved toward the voice, Brynn feeling instant shame. Jamie was holding on to the pool ledge and staring up at them with frightened eyes while Candy dog-paddled behind her.

"Nothing, baby. Go on and swim."

The child looked doubtfully between them. A faint ringing could be heard inside the house, and Brynn seized on the distraction gratefully.

"The phone," she said, turning toward the French doors.

"No, I'll get it."

He strode inside before she could move, leaving her to settle back into her chair with tears coating her eyes.

Father, am I being selfish? Should I put Jamie's needs before my own feelings?

If only He would answer audibly so she couldn't confuse her own desires with His, but God didn't work that way. She did have, however, an undeniably strong sense that her decision was the right one.

When the door opened and Michael exited, cordless phone in hand, she glared at him, ready for battle. But the expression on his face blew every wisp of anger away.

"Brynn, could you come here a minute?"

She immediately complied, drawing very near to him and gazing upward anxiously.

"It's Mrs. Boyd," he said, too quietly for the girls to hear. "Chad's in trouble. He's at a neighbor's house and they're threatening to call the police."

Chapter Thirteen

After a hurried phone call, Michael and Brynn dropped off the girls at Candy's house and picked up Mrs. Boyd. She told them the address of the neighbor, Mr. Dunlap, and explained he'd found Chad loitering in his garage and believed the boy intended to steal something.

Michael parked the van at a two-story white frame house, and Brynn worried about the elderly lady as they guided her toward the front door. She appeared exceptionally frail.

"I'm not what he needs," Mrs. Boyd said as Michael rang the doorbell. "The school was right to go after a court order to put him in foster care. He'd be better off in the state's care than with an old woman like me."

"Please don't talk that way," Brynn soothed. "You've done a wonderful job with Chad. I'm sure this is all a misunderstanding."

Michael gave her a look that said she'd gone over the line, but she cut her eyes away from him and tightened her lips. He didn't know. Until she heard otherwise, she'd believe in Chad's innocence.

A plump, pleasant-faced woman met them at the door and introduced herself as Jean Dunlap. Her husband, Mac, was scarecrow thin and looked considerably older, with deep lines crisscrossing his tanned skin like a map.

"Come on in," he said, his brilliant blue eyes including them all, and ushered them into a small living room. "The boy's back in the kitchen with Jeremy, eating cookies. Thought we'd talk a spell before bringing him in here."

Mrs. Boyd settled her purse in her lap and faced his voice. "It was good of you to call us, Mac."

"Well now, Leta, if it hadn't been your grandson I would've gone straight to the police. But I knew there must be good in him if he was yours."

"I've known Mac since he was a boy," Mrs. Boyd explained to her companions. "Just what did Chad do?"

"It's not so much what he did as what he was up to. There's been a passel of robberies around here, don't you know, and some of us have been thinking it's a homeless person or a bunch of boys up to no good. Nothing much has been taken. A couple of half-full paint cans at the Robertsons', a pair of garden shears at the Beasleys'. When I found your boy, I asked him what he was doing, and he couldn't give me a good answer. So I put two and two together."

"I didn't do nothing," Chad said from the doorway, cookie crumbs dusting his chin. A tall teenager stood behind him—Jeremy, Brynn supposed. "I was just looking around."

Michael stiffened. "Looking around in someone else's garage without permission? Don't you know trespassing is wrong?"

"I didn't have nothing else to do," Chad said sullenly.

Brynn could feel Michael bristle. "That's not an acceptable answer."

"No, it's not," Mrs. Boyd agreed. "What's wrong with you, child? You know better."

Jeremy said, "Tell 'em what you told me."

Chad gave him an icy glare and tightened his fists.

"Please, Chad," Brynn entreated, her heart hammering in fear for the boy.

His eyes flitted in her direction, then down. "They made me," he admitted grudgingly.

"He's talking about Jimmy Chance's group," Jeremy supplied. "They're gang wannabes. Think they live in the city and want people to be scared of 'em, stupid baby seventh-graders. You got to steal something to get initiated into the group."

Brynn couldn't believe what she was hearing. "You were trying to join a gang, Chad? By stealing?"

"No! I been telling and telling them I don't want to be a member, but they said they was gonna beat me up if I didn't do it."

"Why were they so anxious to have you join?" Michael asked skeptically.

"They wanted me to be their lookout for when they took stuff. But I wasn't going to take nothing from Mr. Dunlap. I decided not to."

"It's true he was on his way out of the garage when I found him," their host said, "and he didn't have anything on him."

"Were those the boys I saw you with at the school fair?" Michael asked, and Chad nodded.

Brynn's attention sharpened. "You know who they are?"

"I could describe them, but I don't know their names."

Mr. Dunlap scooted forward and clasped his hands between his knees. "I'll tell you what. If you can persuade Chad to talk to the police about them boys, it would be good for all of 'em. Maybe keep 'em out of bigger trouble."

"They'll beat me up!" Chad burst out. "I can't say nothing!"

"No one's going to hurt you," Michael said firmly. "The police won't say who told them."

Chad's angry, desperate gaze wandered from him to Brynn, who longed to shelter him in her arms and protect him from all of his problems and the rough world in which he lived. Finally his eyes moved on to his grandmother, who pulled a tissue from her purse with trembling fingers.

"It's the right thing to do," Brynn said softly.

Lowering his lashes, Chad said he would.

Brynn watched Michael's eyes as he looked at the boy. Michael loved the child. She was certain of it. Michael wouldn't be so disappointed in him tonight if he didn't care.

"I feel sorry for Mrs. Boyd," Brynn said after Michael had dropped off Chad and his grandmother. "She was so upset tonight."

"You can understand how she'd feel that way. Her grandson broke the law. Even if he didn't steal anything *this* time, he trespassed."

"But only because he was afraid," she rushed to say. "Those boys bullied him into participating. He wasn't going to take anything. Not ever."

"So *he* said."

"And I believe him. Don't you, Michael?"

"I don't know what to believe about that boy."

His voice sounded tight, and she stared at his profile in dismay. "Are you angry with him?"

He cut a look at her. They were headed toward the countryside and no streetlights lit the road, but she could see his distress in the glow of the dashboard.

"Aren't you? After all we've done for him, this is the thanks we get?"

"You make it sound as though he directed his actions at us, when he was only responding to a threat."

"How do we know he was afraid? Because he said so?"

"Oh, Michael, don't you see how guilty he's been

feeling, how moody? Remember the day of the school picnic, when he worried out loud about God being angry with him? He was sending a message for help.'' She paused, recalling her private conversation with the child. ''I knew something was wrong. I should've pursued it.''

Moving swiftly, he took her hand tightly in his. ''I will *not* listen to you blame yourself. If Chad was afraid, he should have asked for protection.''

Brynn wanted to act casual about his gesture—she knew he meant it casually—but the feeling of strength around her fingers, the press of his skin against hers, heightened her pulse so alarmingly she feared he might sense it through her palm. Thank goodness it was too dark for him to see her face. She was blushing like a twelve-year-old.

When she trusted herself to speak, she said, ''Maybe he didn't think we could help him. He's had a tough life, losing his mother so young.'' She swallowed. ''And never having a father.''

She chanced a look at him, a wish suddenly bubbling to her mind. Chad needed a father badly, and Michael would make a perfect foster father.

The more she thought about it, the better her solution seemed. Chad and Jamie already acted like brother and sister, and Barbara was fond of him. Surely the new nanny would be, too. And the boy worshiped Michael.

But it was unlikely Michael would volunteer to take on a foster child, and she dared not suggest it.

Such a large responsibility would have to come from his own mind.

With a little help from God, it *could* happen. She'd make it a matter of prayer.

"I'm not downplaying his disadvantages," he said, and it took her a minute to recall what he was talking about. "But you've given him so much over the past few months, and I've acted as his Big Brother. We've provided a taste of normal family life. And instead of trusting us to help him, he does something like this. This is how boys get started in crime. One little step at a time."

"Before you send him off to prison for life," Brynn said, her tone dangerously quiet, "maybe you'll recall he's only eight years old. He doesn't think like a rational adult. And maybe he needs more than just a *taste* of normal family life. Maybe he needs it all the time."

"I agree," Michael said as he withdrew his hand to signal a right turn.

Brynn blinked. "You do?"

"His grandmother sounded pretty sincere about handing him over to the foster care system. I think she's right."

"I'm glad to hear you say that."

It was his turn to act surprised. "I thought you were against it because of the insecurity you experienced."

"I've reconsidered. I think it all depends on who Chad ends up with. If he finds a family who loves him enough to keep him long-term...maybe someone who will want to adopt him..."

Michael nodded. "That would be good for him. Let's hope for the best."

I'll be doing more than hoping, Brynn thought.

The first thing she planned to do tomorrow was talk to Mrs. Boyd and ask her to delay her decision in giving Chad over to the foster system. She wanted to give Michael more time. If he didn't think of taking the boy on his own, she *would* suggest it.

When Brynn, Jamie and Candy went to pick up Chad for church the next day, Michael told himself he shouldn't be surprised, but he was. That Brynn persisted in trying to help the boy had long since ceased to amaze him, but he thought Chad might refuse to attend, given the trauma of last night.

But no such luck. Although Candy was going home with her parents after church, the boy was coming to Michael's as always, expecting a takeout luncheon of Chinese, pizza, subs.... Michael had come to enjoy surprising them with something different every week, never dropping a hint as to what it might be.

Today he wandered restlessly through the empty house. If left to himself, he'd not have invited the boy. But Brynn wanted him to come, and she was going to be here only a little while longer.

The thought sent a shaft of loneliness through him.

That was why he allowed Brynn to go on as usual,

because he wanted to please her. After she left, the Chad problem would go away.

He was sure it would.

Melancholy deepening, he went to the few framed photos of Genna he'd kept on display in various rooms, then paged through the family photo album for more. His wife had had such *hope* in her eyes.

In a final act of misery, he climbed the attic stairs and opened the cedar chest he kept for his daughter: a favorite sweater of Genna's, her high school yearbooks, a poem she had written for Jamie on the child's first birthday. Little tokens to remind the girl of the mother she barely knew.

He buried his face in a soft flannel gown that had been his wife's favorite while she nursed Jamie. "I'm so sorry," he whispered.

Though he felt grief, the usual rush of desolation failed to appear. Slowly he replaced the items and locked the chest.

This was what he feared would happen, that he'd gradually become numb to the tragedy, that her loss and his role in it would cease to shake him.

He was no better a man than his father. In many ways, he was worse.

He dragged himself down the stairs and to his Audi. Life went on, didn't it? And now life said it was time to get lunch.

When Brynn swept into the kitchen after church looking as young and tender as a spring morning, the two children crowding past her, he felt a sense of sorrow that came close to undoing him. The sadness was for more than the coming separation from Brynn, he told himself. It was for a way of life forever beyond him, one in which the future throbbed with innocence and promise.

"Lasagna!" Chad cried as he raced into the kitchen. "My favorite!"

"Every food is your favorite," Jamie said with a grown-up sigh.

"Yeah, but lasagna especially."

"You sound pretty chipper after last night," Michael said to Chad. It was a childish strike, he knew, but he couldn't look at the boy without tasting disappointment.

The brightness faded from Chad's face. Immediately, Brynn glided her fingers through the child's hair.

"Why don't you two go to the playroom for a few minutes while I throw a salad together?" As soon as the children ran from the room, she turned to Michael, fire in her eyes. "Aren't you going to give him a chance?"

"He's had plenty of chances."

"Everyone makes mistakes. Even you."

Michael turned his back to her and with deliberate movements began to remove glasses from the cabinet.

Her fingers brushed his shoulder so briefly, so lightly, that he glanced to see if he'd imagined the contact. The sympathy in her eyes told him everything he needed to know.

"I'm sorry, Michael. I didn't mean—"

"I know you didn't. Don't worry about it."

While he put ice in the glasses and set the table, she pulled a pre-made salad packet from the refrigerator, emptied it into a bowl, then added cherry tomatoes and tossed the salad with oil and vinegar.

The silence was deafening.

When she called the children to lunch, he felt relieved, even if it did mean seeing Chad. As the boy entered the kitchen, his walk slowed and his face grew sober, and the looks he dashed toward Michael were covert and worried.

"Can I say grace?" Chad asked when they were seated around the table. It was a request he'd never made before, that ritual usually falling to Jamie. The table blessing was a tradition Michael had continued out of respect for Genna.

Appearing surprised, Brynn assured him he could, then bowed her head. Jamie made a great show of folding her hands and tilting her neck skyward, her eyes squeezed shut except when she peeped at Michael. His daughter could make him smile no matter what. Heart rushing with love for her, he lowered his lashes and waited.

"Hello, heavily Father," Chad began, so loudly that Jamie snickered. "Thanks for this food, especially the lasagna. God bless Grandma, God bless Brynn—"

"That's for night prayers, silly," Jamie whispered, and Brynn immediately shushed her.

Michael was consumed by a sudden need to cough.

"And God bless *Jamie,* even if she does butt in on my talking to You, and God bless Mr. Hudson and help him not to be mad at me anymore so he'll want to go with us to see the fish, Amen."

In the sudden quiet, three pairs of eyes bored into Michael's.

"Fish?" he said.

"Have some salad," Brynn said, passing him the bowl, making an effort at normalcy that he saw through like glass. "You remember, Michael. All of the second grades are going to the Tennessee Aquarium in Chattanooga for their end-of-the-year outing."

He vaguely recalled agreeing to something months ago, back in the comfortable days of winter when the approach of June had seemed as far away as eternity. Something about playing chaperone to—was it over a *hundred* second graders?

What could he have been thinking?

"In buses?" he blurted.

"Well…yes," Brynn admitted.

"Yay, buses!" Jamie said, clapping her hands.

"But you're not even in school yet," he told his daughter.

"Mrs. Jewell gave us permission to bring her if you'd come," Brynn reminded him, trying to distract him by heaping a square of lasagna on his plate. "Male chaperones are rare, you know."

"Huh. Imagine that."

He couldn't do this. There had to be some way out that wouldn't make it seem as if he were breaking his word.

"One of the privileges of owning your own business is that you can take time off sometimes, isn't it?" she said, bright as a mother trying to convince a child that the dentist was a fun place to visit.

Michael speared a tomato into his mouth while he thought furiously.

"He doesn't want to go," Chad declared, and scuffed back his chair to run for the front door. "He hates me!"

Brynn flashed him a devastated look as she raced after the boy, and Jamie followed, yelling Chad's name.

Michael stared at their abandoned plates as he listened to the voices in the hallway. Brynn and Jamie were begging Chad to return to the table. The boy was asserting he intended to walk home.

Michael closed his eyes for a moment, then walked slowly into the hall.

"Come back to the table, Chad. You know it's too far to walk."

"I don't want to eat nothing."

"Then I'll take you home. Let's go."

"Michael!" Brynn cried.

Chad's hands knotted into fists, and his eyes filled with tears. "Why are you so mad at me? God forgave me for what I did!"

"*God* forgave you?" From the corner of his eye

he sensed Brynn's blazing glance, but he wouldn't look at her.

"Yeah, because I asked Him to and promised not to do it again." The boy looked desperately at Brynn. "At least, she told me He forgave me and still loves me, and Mr. Mandon said it at Sunday school. But maybe He doesn't!"

Something within Michael melted, and he responded instinctively to the child's distress, crouching on one knee and gripping both of Chad's arms firmly. His own faith might be in tatters, but a boy like this needed something to keep him on the straight path.

"You're really going to stay away from those boys?"

"Yeah," he said, a spark of hope in his eyes. "They stink."

"And you know what you did was wrong?"

Holding his breath, Michael could almost read the thoughts passing behind the child's eyes—it wasn't my fault, I was afraid, all the things that spelled danger because it would mean he refused to take responsibility for his actions. And then Chad's eyes drooped.

"Yeah," he said. "I should have told somebody."

"Okay, then." He gave the boy a little shake. "If God's not mad at you, how can I be?"

Chad's smile was so bright he could almost feel his skin tanning. "Then you'll go with us?"

Michael's eyes lingered on Brynn. "You don't think I'd let you have all that fun without me, do you?"

When he stood, it wasn't Chad's and Jamie's approval he basked in, but Brynn's. She threw her arms around him in an impulsive embrace, which he returned with an exuberant feeling so natural and sweet that he was surprised when tears stung at the backs of his lids.

Chapter Fourteen

Genna would have hated this, Michael thought as he parked his van and stared at the line of yellow buses waiting in front of the school. Probably she'd have put her foot down about allowing Jamie on a school bus. The ugly yellow tubes were always getting into wrecks on the news, and they really should be equipped with seat belts. If anything happened today, he'd feel doubly guilty.

Maybe someday he'd be able to travel without thinking about vehicular accidents.

He wasn't sure he was up to this excursion, but there was no backing out now. Brynn and Jamie were already climbing out of the van, and somewhere in that crowd Chad was expecting them.

He owed this day to his daughter. Unwilling though he was, he'd have to begin advertising for Brynn's replacement soon, and the child would have to know the truth.

It saddened him that he couldn't persuade Brynn to stay, but she remained firmly fixed on her new job. He hated to imagine how Jamie would face her loss. He hated to think how *he* was going to deal with it. The house would seem empty without her.

But in one way it would be a relief. She constantly tempted him from the sorrow he owed his wife. Every gesture she made, every outrageous plan she hatched, even the tilt of her head when she fixed those quicksilver eyes on him, beckoned him to renewed life.

And there he could not, *would* not go.

They found Mrs. Jewell's class easily enough, and he greeted her in his best soothing manner. She looked harried already, her eyes sharp and restless behind large spectacles.

"I'm glad you're here," she said to him and Brynn. "Chad's in a mood this morning."

"Oh, no," Brynn said. "Any idea why?"

"One never knows with that child."

She could at least pretend to have a good attitude about the kid, Michael thought. She never gave him a break. Dismissing the woman with a pleasant nod, he took Brynn's elbow and led her past hordes of ecstatic faces until they found Chad, who hardly cracked a smile when he saw them.

They found seats near the back of the bus, one behind the other. Jamie, perhaps sensitive to Chad's mood, insisted on sitting beside the boy. That left Brynn to join him, something he didn't mind in the least despite a single faint tug of guilt.

While they talked comfortably of inconsequential matters, both of them carefully avoiding the coming separation, he could scarcely keep his gaze from her delicate skin and clear, intelligent eyes. When she laughed she abandoned herself to the laughter, color rushing to her cheeks and mischief lighting her face. But when she glanced at the pair sitting in front of them, her expression grew solemn, and he found the transition fascinating.

"Mrs. Jewell was right about Chad," she told him. There was no need for her to lower her voice; the bus was too noisy for the children to hear. "Something's wrong. He's hardly talking to Jamie."

"The boy has the temperament of a pogo stick," he said, anxious to return amusement to her eyes. "There's no reason why he shouldn't be happy. Those boys won't bother him—the police reassured us on that. Don't worry, Jamie will loosen him up."

"I hope you're right. Maybe he's experiencing delayed trauma from talking to a policeman."

"That wouldn't be a bad thing. He had a close call. The scare should make him think twice about getting into trouble again."

She remained quiet for a moment. "You sound as if you're still angry at him in spite of what you said the other day."

"I've never been angry," he replied, then wondered if that was true. "More disappointed than anything." Wanting her to believe him, he added, "Who am I to disapprove, anyway? I was no angel as a boy."

He was pleased to see this immediately caught her interest. "You were a troublemaker? I don't believe it."

"I was the terror of sixth grade," he asserted.

"Say it isn't true!" Her teasing smile delighted him.

"Sorry, but it is. After my father left us, I got the mistaken notion that I was the head of the home, since I was the oldest boy. At first Mom let me get away with things. I guess she was too shaken emotionally to deal with me. But later, when she tried to grab control back, she and I locked horns like a couple of rams."

"The poor woman. What sort of things did you do?"

"Nothing too serious by today's standards. I tried to boss my younger brothers around, which they resented thoroughly. Once I charged a bow-and-arrow set down at O'Leedy's, a general store that no longer exists, by the way. I thought I'd be able to protect the family with it, but Mom made me take it back. A major humiliation for a boy who thought he was a man."

"Even then you were trying to keep your loved ones from harm," she said, an admiring light in her eyes that made him uncomfortable. "Is your mother still living?"

"No, she died a few years ago." The words brought a distant ache he hadn't felt in a while. Talking to Brynn had stirred up old memories, and he was surprised to realize how many of them were good ones. "At least she had a chance to know Genna. That's why I came back to Sherwin Falls. I wanted to share my family with her."

"Did you ever try to find your father?"

"Three years after he left, we got word through a neighbor that he was killed at a construction accident. We never learned if drinking was a factor."

"I'm sorry."

"Don't be. There was no chance of a relationship with him, anyway."

She shook her head. "What about your brothers? Do you see them?"

He felt a flash of annoyance and quelled it. Brynn's interest was genuine, not idle curiosity.

"It's been a few years since I saw Ted. Last I heard, he was living in California and producing documentaries. Davy's a fireman in Alabama. He's married and has a couple of kids. I haven't seen him since Genna's funeral."

He waited for the expected spear of pain that accompanied his wife's name. A blaze of anxiety came when he felt nothing.

"Then you're overdue a couple of visits," she said in pert tones.

Still rattled, he said offhandedly, "Actually, we don't have all that much in common."

"That can't be true, not when you shared the same history. If I had a family, I'd annoy them to death with my presence. They wouldn't be able to get away from me."

"No one could possibly want to get away from

you," he said sincerely, and was treated to another blush.

The time passed faster than he thought possible. Before he knew it, they were skirting the Chattanooga side of Lookout Mountain, then exiting off Interstate 24 onto Fourth Street. A couple more blocks and they had arrived. The children and adults piled off the bus, most of them craning their necks upward to view the impressive glass-and-brick structure standing guard over the Tennessee River.

Over the next few hours, they laid seige to the aquarium in regiments worthy of one of those Civil War battles the Chattanoogans he knew were always going on about. After the children marched past the gift shops and back onto the bricked walk outside, they gathered in chaperoned groups to eat lunch. He couldn't help noticing Chad ate only a couple of bites of his sandwich before rolling the bread into a ball and dropping it back into his bag.

"Are you sick?" he asked the boy. "Usually you have the appetite of an alligator."

"Not hungry," Chad mumbled, leaning back on his hands and scanning the sky.

"Are you going to tell us what's wrong?" Brynn's tone was quiet enough that the other children couldn't hear—they were chattering like mad bluejays anyway—but unusually firm. He felt proud of her. The boy didn't need to be coddled when he acted like this.

The child looked obstinate for a minute, then said, "Grandma's sick."

"Oh, Chad! Why didn't she call me?" Brynn said.

"She just went to the doctor yesterday and he told her she needed somebody to take care of her, so she called Aunt Grace. She said she'd take care of Grandma, but she couldn't watch me, too. So I got to go live with some friends somewhere."

Michael's stomach tightened as Brynn embraced the boy and whispered, "Oh, sweet Chad."

Jamie rose to her knees and shuffled closer, her face dark as an approaching storm. "What friends are you staying with?"

As Brynn released him, Chad shrugged his shoulders and looked at the pavement.

"You could live with us," Jamie said. "Couldn't he, Daddy?"

Michael felt the world stop. Three pairs of eyes swung toward him, all of them hopeful.

They must be kidding.

The children he could understand, but why was Brynn looking at him expectantly? Surely she knew how he felt about taking a potential problem into his home. He hadn't made any secret of it.

"It doesn't work like that, honey," he said, trying to soften his words with a laugh. "These things are complicated. There are lists and lists of people waiting to help children like Chad. People with training who love big families. I wouldn't be surprised if he winds up living on a farm with horses and cows...."

He trailed away as Brynn turned from him. She had never looked so disappointed in anyone, at least not in his presence. His stomach knotted tighter.

Jamie stood, scowling. "But I want him to live with *us!*"

"Oh, never mind," Chad said. "Who cares."

Michael reached toward him. "Of course we care. After you get settled with your new family, we'll have you over for swimming and picnics and all the pizza you can eat."

"No, you won't," the boy responded. "I'll probably be a hundred miles away and living with strangers who'll hate me, and I won't even get to be in Brynn's third grade."

"Huh?" Jamie put her thumb in her mouth.

When Brynn's horrified eyes flew to his, Michael hurriedly tried to change the subject. "What was your favorite fish in the aquarium, Jamie?"

"I don't remember no fish's names." Jamie's chin began to tremble as she turned back to her nanny. "Are you going to third grade?"

Brynn moistened her lips. "We'll talk about this later, okay? Chad, who told you?"

"Mrs. Jewell. Some of the kids asked who was gonna be teaching third grade next year, because we heard Mrs. Stovameer was retiring."

Jamie tapped Brynn's knee demandingly. "You leaving me?"

Pulling her closer, Brynn said, "Honey, you knew I was applying for a job and couldn't stay forever. But I'll come to see you, I promise. We can continue going to church, if your dad doesn't mind. We'll still be together a lot."

"No!"

When Jamie shoved away from her, Michael felt Brynn's pain as if it were his own. He grabbed his daughter's hand and forced her into his lap. She struggled without tears, silently pushing and pushing at his arms, but he held on.

The other children watched this scene with interest, but Michael barely noticed. He tried to catch Brynn's eye, but her head was bowed and she wouldn't look at either of them.

The day had held such promise, but now it was ruined, Brynn thought as she moved numbly to the final step of the day: the IMAX theater. Chad stared straight ahead like a stoic, Jamie was quiet, ominously so, and Michael looked terrible. One small part of her felt glad, because he *should* feel badly for brushing off Chad's hopes with stories about horses and barns—mere crumbs for the boy's sorrow and loneliness.

But she couldn't blame Michael for his feelings. He doubtless still viewed the child as a bad influence on his daughter despite how much better, how much happier, she'd been since knowing him.

Even so, Brynn had nothing to say to him as they waited in line. Fortunately Michael didn't seem talkative, either.

She had her own guilt to bear. She felt like a traitor for accepting the teaching position. Poor Jamie. The girl must feel as if she were losing two of her friends at the same time. Brynn didn't know how to help her.

At the entrance to the theater an attendant handed each of them an oversize pair of 3-D glasses. They marched up the stairs and filed down one of the rows near the top.

The film was about a young girl living on a space station, and Brynn relaxed as she sensed Jamie's involvement. On her other side, Chad slouched and kicked the chair in front of him until its occupant, an irate red-haired girl, turned and hissed at him to stop.

Afterward, the children were herded into the rest rooms in groups. Brynn and Michael parted to mind their charges, and by the time they rejoined each other in the lobby, bedlam was in full force.

While Brynn stooped to hear Chad's comments on the movie—he thought there should have been more boys in it—Jamie wandered to her father's side. One of the girls in Brynn's group held up a split fingernail, and she obligingly searched her purse for clippers. Finishing the emergency repair, she straightened, her glance finding Michael at once. He was making idle chatter with Mrs. Jewell, winning her over with his charm. The aging woman actually smiled at something he said.

Brynn's gaze fell as she automatically searched for Jamie. The girl was not standing beside her father now.

Brynn couldn't spot her anywhere.

Oh no, Lord, not again.

Heart drumming in her ears, she pushed her way to Michael. "Where's Jamie?"

He blanched. "I thought she was with you."

"She said she wanted to be with her daddy. I watched until she reached you." Someone tugged on her sleeve. "Not now, Chad."

"I just saw Jamie go outside with some lady!" he shouted. "I yelled at her to stop, but she didn't hear me!"

As her eyes met Michael's, visions of kidnappers immediately flooded her mind. There had been a couple of kidnappings in Chattanooga reported on the news. What a perfect opportunity to grab a child and not be noticed. She knew he was thinking the same.

"God help us," he murmured, and sprinted through the lobby and out the glass doors.

Brynn followed, hardly able to breathe. The look on Michael's face had stamped panic all the way through to her bones.

"Brynn!" Chad called behind her.

She turned and saw the boy pushing through the doors. "Honey, go back inside with the others where it's safe," she told him.

"I want to help find Jamie!"

His ashen skin and panic-filled eyes dissolved her resistance. She stepped back a few paces, grabbed his hand and ran forward.

Trying desperately to catch up with Michael, she was only able to keep him in sight among the pedestrians. Truth was, she could have tracked him by his voice. Every time he called Jamie's name, his frantic tones twisted her heart.

"Is that her?" Chad said, pulling her hand and pointing down the sidewalk.

She stopped and saw a tall woman hurrying toward the downtown area, a little girl clutching the handle of her purse. For a second Brynn's heart stood still, but she realized the child's hair was too light, her clothes different. Before she could put voice to the thought, Chad tugged her forward.

"That's not her. Jamie's skinnier."

They continued after Michael, heading toward the parking lot. She could see the buses from Sherwin Falls Elementary lined up one beside the other. The sight struck her as unbearably poignant. She didn't want to reenter those yellow dinosaurs until everything was all right. She could not imagine returning to Sherwin Falls without Jamie.

She prayed as she ran. If the girl was lost, Brynn would carry the grief of it to her grave. But Michael...surely he wouldn't be asked to give up the one being who kept his heart open to the world and to love. He'd already been hurt too much. How could he live with this?

The architect had reached the far end of the parking lot by the time she and Chad were halfway past the endless rows of cars. He leaned beyond the sidewalk and peered from one end of the street to the other, his arms rising and falling once in angry bewilderment.

Please God, she begged. *Please don't let this horrible thing happen. He won't be able to bear it.*

Through burning, dry eyes Michael saw Brynn and Chad approaching. His heart had slowed to a dull thud that vibrated through his body with every beat. Consciously he forced all emotion from his features. If he gave voice or expression to an inkling of his fear, he'd fall apart completely.

How can you do this to me, God? Haven't you taken enough already?

Panicked though he was, he heard his prayer with shock.

Why was he blaming God when he didn't believe in Him?

Knowing his voice would tremble, he whipped out his cellular from his pocket and pounded 911 before Brynn reached him. Even so, she and the boy arrived before he finished explaining to the police dispatcher, and he tried to take comfort from the hand she rested on his shoulder.

"We're going to find her," Brynn said, her reddened eyes holding his with absolute certainty.

He wanted to believe her, but couldn't. "I told the police we'd meet them at the theater," he said, his voice sounding like a stranger's. "We'd better get back."

"Can't we pray to God to find Jamie?" Chad said.

Brynn's glance cut from the child to him, a thousand emotions reflecting through her eyes. He felt her instant agreement, then the doubts.

He remembered how he used to think, back when he believed in a heavenly Architect. How he'd pray that God's will be done, giving Him an out in case He didn't come through.

Right now Brynn would be wondering if prayer

would help or hurt him, because it might *not* be God's will to give him back what he needed most in the world.

Feeling Chad's gaze piercing him, he reluctantly looked at the boy. Although the afternoon sun caused the child to squint, his fear and concern were as real as Brynn's and his own. With sudden insight he saw how fragile the boy's faith nested within, that what he said and how he acted in the next few moments could spell confirmation for that belief or disaster.

He didn't want that kind of responsibility. Not now, not when his heart wanted to stop beating if it meant going on without Jamie. Why should he care if the boy believed in God or not?

But he did. It was important for Chad to see order in the universe, to believe there was a loving Father who cared about him and wanted him to grow into a kind and gentle man, one who recognized that goodness and empathy were the keystones of a well-lived life.

If it's important for him, a voice whispered, *why isn't it important for you?*

He couldn't believe he was thinking about spiritual matters when his daughter was missing.

"Let's get closer to the IMAX so we'll be there when the police arrive. You can pray there."

Before crossing the street, he drew them between the last two cars in the lot and nodded for Chad to pray. No sense in making a spectacle of themselves. People both young and old were huddled near the glass doors of the theater, watching them with worry.

Mrs. Jewell leaned from the door to express her concern.

"We've called the police," he shouted back.

"We're going to pray!" Chad added, making Michael want to cringe.

"That's a good idea," Mrs. Jewell called, her voice shaking. "We'll pray, too."

Michael nodded numbly, thinking she meant the words as a generic sentiment. But as he watched she returned inside and, in a voice loud enough to be heard across the street, ordered the class of second graders to close their eyes and pray if they wanted to, that she certainly intended to do so and believed many of the other teachers and chaperones would want to, as well.

She was probably breaking all kinds of government regulations in giving those instructions, but he had a strong feeling no one would object. As he saw heads bowing, he felt connected to them in a wonderful way, as though their souls were binding together in mutual concern and hope for his daughter.

A rush of warmth filled him as Brynn's and Chad's hands slipped into his, then joined to make a circle. The ravaged state of his heart remained, but he knew he wasn't alone.

Chad prayed quickly, asking God to help them find Jamie. Brynn's prayer was just as brief and sincere. Michael thanked them when they finished.

"Aren't you going to pray?" Chad asked.

He almost balked. But it took only a little effort to mumble the words for help, and by the time he was finished he felt a trace of comfort, some of which came in the form of memory. In the past he'd found solace in prayer, and for just a moment it seemed the rift between belief and unbelief had never happened.

But it had. Genna's death and the boggling grief and guilt of it freshly flooded his veins. And now Jamie was gone. The pain nearly tore him in two.

Three police cars pulled against the curb, and Michael hurried toward the first officer to emerge. The shock of so much manpower increased his fears. The police were taking this seriously. The senior officer, a squarely built man named Justin Brock, instructed the officers in the first car to search the closest buildings and streets; two were dispatched to the theater to gather more information.

Officer Brock squatted to Chad's eye level. "Are you sure you saw her leave with a woman?"

"Jamie was right behind her," Chad said.

"What did the woman look like?"

The boy's expression grew fearful. "I don't remember too good. She was tall. I think she had long hair."

"Brown? Blond?"

Chad shook his head. "Can't remember."

"Which way did she go?"

"I don't know!"

Michael moved impatiently. "We're wasting time. Can't we get in your patrol car and search the streets? They could be heading out of town by now."

"Sir, we've got patrols doing that already. The

best thing you can do is go inside the theater and wait.''

''I can't do that.''

Officer Brock gave him a steady look. ''I'd feel the same way if it was my kid, but—'' A sudden mechanical noise inside his car caught his attention and he stooped inside the vehicle. Seconds later he swung back. ''Step in, sir. They've found someone that might be your daughter, and we'll need you to confirm.''

''Is she all right?'' Brynn asked anxiously, climbing into the backseat beside him with Chad following.

''I believe so, ma'am,'' he said, hitting the siren and pulling into traffic. ''If we've got the right one.''

Chad scooted forward and patted the mesh separating front and back seats, his eyes round as Moon Pies. ''Cool!''

Several blocks down, the cruiser swerved into a parking garage where a police car already rested, its light flashing soundlessly and casting blue hues over a pair of officers and a woman with long, curly hair who crouched beside a weeping child. With a gasp of relief and thankfulness, Michael recognized Jamie. He tried to bound out of the car, and realized he couldn't until the officer opened the door for him. ''That's her,'' he nearly shouted, hardly registering the echoing cries of Brynn and Chad. ''Hurry and let me out!''

The instant he reached Jamie, Michael grabbed his child and lifted her in his arms, rocking her from side to side while she clung to him tightly. Rising, the woman looked bewildered, her eyes moving from Michael to the girl, then to Brynn when she joined them.

"I don't understand," the stranger told him. "She thought I was her mother." Worriedly, she added, "I hope you don't think I took her. *She* followed *me.* I didn't know she was behind me until just a few minutes ago. As soon as I realized it, I had the parking attendant call the police."

Michael couldn't answer. His eyes were squeezed shut as he murmured comforts to Jamie, one hand cupping her head against his shoulder. Beside him he heard Brynn say quietly, "It's not your fault. Her mother died recently, and you resemble her."

He opened his eyes and saw the woman's distressed look melt to sympathy. "Oh, my, the poor baby. To lose her mother so young. It's a hard world sometimes, isn't it?"

"Yes," Brynn said. "It is." She touched the stranger's arm briefly. "But not all the time. Thank you for staying with her."

Distantly Michael registered that the woman must be telling the truth, but a part of him resented her for taking his baby away, however unintentionally. Why hadn't she noticed Jamie following her sooner? He knew he wasn't being rational, and he was grateful Brynn was able to be civil to her on their behalf.

"Well, I wouldn't have left her," the stranger said. "I have two sons of my own. But I *was* wondering what I would do if the officers wanted to take her to the station. I didn't think I should abandon her, but to tell the truth I'm expected at home, so I'm glad you found her quickly. You think she'll be all right now?''

"I'm sure she will."

Michael hoped Brynn was right. Jamie's anguish shook him with its depth. She seemed inconsolable.

After a few additional words with the officers, the woman walked away.

Gradually Jamie's wails diminished to heaving sobs. Michael became aware that Brynn had moved near and was rubbing her back gently. At the same time Chad patted Jamie's arm with earnest regularity.

"It's all right," the boy said. "You didn't get lost. We found you. And *I* helped." Michael felt a tug at his trousers. "Didn't I?"

"You sure did," he said, feeling closer to the child at that moment than he ever had. To his daughter, he murmured, "Why, baby? Why did you run from us?"

The child shuddered in his arms. "She looked like my mommy."

"Jamie, Jamie," Michael said, sliding her to the ground and kneeling to her height, his heart breaking. "You've got to let your mother go, baby. She's gone."

If only *I* could accept that, he thought with a painful glance at Brynn, whose eyes had filled with tears.

"But won't she come back?"

"No, she can't come back, not ever, but I know she's watching out for you."

"Watching me? From where, Daddy?"

He slowly turned his eyes to Brynn again. "You know, sweetheart. From heaven."

He heard Brynn's breath catch in her throat. She stood absolutely motionless, as if in fear of disturbing the moment. In her hopeful eyes he read, *Do you really mean it?*

"But you don't believe in heaven," Jamie said.

"I do now."

Squinting her eyes, Jamie pulled back from him. "Why?"

He grabbed her up in his arms. This time his gaze caught Brynn's and held. *Don't expect too much too soon,* he tried to warn her.

"Because I have you," he said.

Chapter Fifteen

On Saturday morning Michael woke later than usual. His sleep had been disturbed by fragmented dreams involving Brynn, Jamie and Genna, which trailed through his waking brain like wisps of fog.

He didn't remember any of the dreams, but he remembered the longing.

Sweeping his arm across Genna's side of the bed, he could almost see her lying there, her anxious eyes watching, always watching him as he awoke. And then a smile would come, as if she'd been afraid he wouldn't awaken at all, as if every day without disaster was a surprise to her. Most mornings he would take her in his arms, hoping to smother her fears with love. Poor sweet Genna. She thought he could protect her from everything.

Oh, God.

The words were a prayer in his mind. A fumbling,

awkward prayer. His praying words had grown rusty. But how easily they had come yesterday when he thought he'd lost Jamie.

Do You really exist, God? Did You keep my daughter from harm? If so, thanks, from the bottom of my heart.

That wasn't very impressive. But if God were listening, at least He'd know the prayer was sincere.

And if God really was there, maybe He'd been behind the healing that had come to his spirit since a certain young lady had barged her way into his home and life.

How his instincts had warred at him for hiring her, because he had been so very determined to remain unhappy.

And just as he'd feared, she made unhappiness impossible.

He slipped out of bed and to the shower. It was time to move on, in more ways than one.

Brynn was sipping coffee at the kitchen table when he entered the kitchen. She looked pretty in a blue-striped knit top and white jeans. Her hair was charmingly disheveled around a flawless face. She didn't have on a speck of makeup and still looked perfect. Seeing her made him ache.

"Good morning," he said brightly, moving toward the coffeemaker.

"Morning," she replied in subdued tones.

He cut her a glance as he poured coffee into his mug. "Bad night?"

She shook her head. "Bad morning."

"What's wrong? Did Jamie have a nightmare?" He sat opposite her and cradled his mug.

"She had a little trouble going to sleep, but she's okay now, sleeping like a log. No, I called Mrs. Boyd this morning, since I know she gets up early. I wanted to catch her when Chad was sleeping so she could talk freely about her illness. It's cancer, Michael."

"I'm so sorry," he said, meaning it.

"There's some hope. She's to have chemotherapy, and her daughter is willing to nurse her through it. But Chad's aunt won't take him. She's never been married and doesn't tolerate children. Not only that, she and Chad's mother didn't get along very well. Mrs. Boyd believes DFCS is the only alternative."

"I know how much you hate the idea of him being in foster care, but I think it could be good for the boy."

"It could be," she said, her eyes distant.

"Matter of fact, I'm surprised they haven't moved to take him before now. It was months ago that the investigation got started."

"I asked her about that. She said the caseworker told her that handing a child over to the state is very serious. Once a child is in the system it's almost impossible to get him out. And since Chad was plainly not in an abusive situation, there was no need to rush. Maybe they were hoping things would work out without their interference."

"And now his grandmother has come to agree with the school that a foster placement is in Chad's best interest," he commented pointedly. If Mrs. Boyd could accept it, surely Brynn would.

"She has no other choice."

He touched her hand briefly in encouragement. "Think about it, Brynn. He'll be away from that neighborhood and those boys who've been bullying him. This move could be just the thing to get his life in order."

Her face changed suddenly, the glow coming back. "And what about you, Michael? Is your life in order now?"

He looked at her in surprise, wondering for an instant if she could read his mind, if somehow she had intuited his thoughts about her. And then he remembered those moments at the aquarium and realized she was referring to that.

"I don't want you making too much of what I said yesterday," he said slowly, wanting to be as honest as he could.

The disappointment in her eyes was immediate. She would never be able to hide anything from him, he thought with pleasure. Brynn's emotions were as transparent as a child's.

"Then you didn't mean what you said to Jamie?" she asked.

"About heaven? Yes, I did."

She stared. "I'm confused."

"What I'm trying to say is that I'm open, not closed as I was before. I'm willing to take instruction, maybe even to start attending church again, but I'm not ready to preach on any street corners, okay?"

"Okay," she said, her lips curling upward. "That seems fair."

"When I thought Jamie had been abducted yesterday, the first thing I did was pray. It started me thinking. Why had I done that after spending the past year absolutely convinced there was no God? Why was prayer such an automatic response?" He paused, wondering what she would do if he suddenly kissed her. "And why are you smiling at me like that?"

"Oh, I was just thinking about something."

He waited. "Well, are you going to tell me or do I have to guess?"

Her smile widened. "I was trying to recall a verse in the Bible where Christ says no one can steal away His children, no matter what, not once they're in His hand. I can't remember it exactly."

"It's from John, chapter ten, I think. 'My sheep hear my voice, and I know them, and they follow me. And I give unto them eternal life; and they shall never perish, neither shall any man pluck them out of my hand.'"

"Michael!" she said, sounding amazed, lights dancing in her eyes. She looked so appealing he had to stop himself from grabbing her.

"All those years memorizing Bible verses to earn a free week in camp," he explained. "You memorize something as a child and you never forget it."

"I think there's more to it than that."

"Oh, you do, do you?"

"Yes, I do. I think God has had you in His hand all along, and you're just coming to realize that."

"You think He's not going to let me go, is that it?"

"Absolutely."

He pretended to shudder. "That's kind of scary."

"I find it comforting! It's hard to imagine going through life without feeling His love, without knowing He's there to guide and strengthen no matter what happens."

"To help you find the good in every situation?" he said with a touch of irony, recalling how angry that statement had once made him.

"To help me find the good," she affirmed.

You're the good, he wanted to tell her, but didn't dare, not yet. He wanted to explore their relationship—if there was to be a relationship. He wasn't sure how he felt about dating again, and he couldn't take it for granted that she returned his feelings, though he'd sensed for some time that she felt *something*—slow and easy, with candlelit dinners, long walks and plenty of time for holding hands and gentle kisses, time to soothe the hurting child within her. She had to know he'd never treat her as Reed Blake had. He wanted her to be sure of that.

Maybe God could help them both. Maybe He was already helping. If the Creator really was guiding their lives, her new job was the best thing that could have happened. But despite his best intentions, he didn't trust himself with her beneath his roof.

He'd been alone such a long time.

"Have you made any plans for Jamie today?" he asked, trying to get his mind settled.

"Not really. After yesterday's excitement I thought a quiet day at home might be in order."

"That's the most sensible thing I've heard all year." Returning to the coffeemaker, he poured them both a fresh cup. "I think I'll take Jamie to her mother's grave site tomorrow afternoon," he added quietly. "She's never been there."

Brynn's eyes softened on him as she sipped. "That's a wonderful idea. I'm not sure how she'll react, but maybe it will help her understand better."

"Maybe it'll help us both understand that life is for the living." He stared at the tan liquid in his mug. "I hope that doesn't sound like I'm lessening what Genna meant to us. She can never be replaced. No human can. But we're not serving her by burying ourselves in grief."

"You don't know how happy it makes me to hear you say that," she said, reaching for his hand, her eyes brimming.

Although the contact was inexpressibly sweet, he could not be less than honest with her. "I guess I'm always going to wonder what I could've done differently, though. To save her life."

"You *must* forgive yourself, Michael. The accident wasn't your fault. Even if it had been, you'd eventually have to come to terms with it and admit that everyone, *everyone,* makes mistakes."

"That may be true, but it's a bitter pill to swallow when your mistake causes someone else to die." He gave the lazy Susan on the tabletop a twirl. "Especially when she expected you to take care of her."

She tilted her head in that adorable way she had. "You know what I believe. Sometimes the only way to work out guilt, real or imagined guilt, is to help other people, to love them sacrificially."

"Is that right."

She hesitated, biting her lower lip. "Michael…"

"Brynn," he teased, staring at her mouth in fascination.

"Are you certain you wouldn't consider giving Chad a home, maybe for just a little while? I'm not talking about taking him as a foster child, because there's no guarantee in the state system that requesting a particular child means you'll get him placed with you. I just mean for an extended visit, to see how things work out, and *then* maybe considering foster parenting." She hesitated. "Or adoption."

Disappointed, he broke off eye contact and leaned back to stare out the window, his hand slipping from hers.

"And if things didn't work out, what then—send him back? We've talked about this already, Brynn. You know how I feel about bringing a child like him into my home."

"Do you really think he's a menace?" she asked earnestly. "Does he strike you as having bad character?"

He thought about it. Although he'd surely been headed for trouble with that gang, the boy had done nothing more mischievous than Michael had in the past. And to be fair, he wasn't sure how he would have reacted at the age of eight if someone had threatened him with a beating. He'd always thought of himself as tough, dealing with an alcoholic father and acting as leader of his brothers. But if he'd felt he was all alone… He just didn't know.

Playing against the minuses were other scenes: Chad sewing on dolls' heads, treating his grandmother with respect, defending Jamie against a bully in the park, worrying about making God angry. And raiding the refrigerator every chance he got. Most of all, his look of pride and relief when Jamie was found.

Feeling Brynn watching him, he caught his smile just in time.

"No, I don't think he's bad. But he's a complication I'm not prepared to bring into our lives. Jamie and I have enough to deal with as it is."

Brynn closed her eyes briefly. "Michael, you'd be good for each other. I know you care for him deeply, or you wouldn't enjoy him so much. I've seen the two of you joking and clowning around. He *needs* you, don't you see? And you need him."

"*I* need *him?*"

"To complete the healing process that God has begun in your life."

He could feel his temper rising. "How do you know that? Are you the voice of God?"

Immediately she lowered her eyes and held up both hands, palms outward. "You're absolutely right. Forgive me, Michael, that was arrogant. I have no business telling you what God wants. Every person needs to decide that prayerfully for himself."

"No offense taken," he said gratefully. She was a passionate woman and he wanted her to be, even if it caused them trouble sometimes. But at least she could see reason.

"I was speaking about what *I* wanted, what *I* thought was best for Chad," she went on heatedly, "and deciding God wanted it, too. That was unforgivable."

"No, it wasn't. I forgive you. I mean, there's nothing to forgive."

"I just thought I should give you one final opportunity—"

"Really, it's all right."

"—before I called Mrs. Boyd."

He waved his hand dismissively as she pushed back her chair, then watched as she rinsed her coffee mug in the sink and placed it in the dishwasher. She seemed very purposeful all of a sudden.

"Why are you calling Mrs. Boyd?"

She turned. "Because I don't want her to give Chad into state custody." She took a deep breath. "I plan to see a lawyer and start adoption procedures right away."

Michael heard the sounds of his perfect new world shattering around his ears.

"*You're* going to *adopt* Chad?"

"If his grandmother will let me."

"Don't be ridiculous! You're just starting your life, Brynn—don't ruin it! You can't possibly realize what a responsibility you'd be taking on!"

"This is what I feel God wants me to do, Michael."

"I can't believe He'd want you to do such an insane thing!"

"Are *you* going to speak for Him now?" she asked quietly, then walked toward him as he flung up his hands helplessly. She stopped only inches from him, within reach, and he longed to hold her until she got her senses back.

"Speaking for God is easy to do, isn't it?" she said with a sad smile. "Don't be angry with me, Michael, please. I could be wrong, I know that. But I'm doing what I think is right. If it's not, then everything will fall through. I really believe that when a person prays for guidance, God listens like a loving Father and answers."

He did reach out to her then, placing one hand on each shoulder. It was a chaste gesture, one she couldn't misinterpret.

"That's good, Brynn, admirable even. Maybe one day I'll come close to your maturity as a Christian, and I'll be able to trust like that, too." He gazed intently into her eyes, hoping with all his life that she would be sensible. "However, I've got to tell you this. If you plan a career as a teacher, you're going to see hundreds of Chads over the years. You can't adopt them all."

"No, I can't," she said, and clasped the hand on her left shoulder with both of hers. "But I intend to adopt the one God has placed in my life and in my heart."

* * *

The next morning Brynn was removing a plate of bacon from the microwave when Michael entered the kitchen wearing a navy pin-striped suit, red tie and a crisp white shirt. She'd never seen him so dressed up and couldn't help staring.

"Daddy!" Jamie cried. The girl had been setting the table, but now the silverware clattered to the plates as she rushed to him. "You look pretty!"

"Not as pretty as the two of you." He raised her for a kiss, his eyes meeting Brynn's as he lowered the child. "Don't look so surprised. I warned you I was willing to try church."

Brynn opened her mouth, then closed it. She wasn't surprised so much as starstruck, and it was with reluctance that she ripped her gaze from his.

"Breakfast is ready," she said in tones so chipper she made herself shiver. She sounded like one of those insane women in commercials who rhapsodized over certain brands of cereal.

"I'm glad you're going with us, Daddy," Jamie said. "Chad'll be fullaberglasted. Want me to call him?"

Michael set the knives, forks and spoons in place. "Oh, let's not spoil the fun," he said lightly.

As the meal progressed, Brynn sensed something was on Michael's mind. She hoped he wasn't thinking about discussing her adoption of Chad, because she wanted to keep her idea secret until she had definite plans in place.

Very quickly she discovered it wasn't that.

"Jamie." His voice sounded more husky than usual, and Brynn felt his nervousness. Apparently his daughter did as well, because she immediately frowned. "On Friday when you ran after that lady, you said you thought she looked like Mommy."

The girl's scowl deepened. Other than a brief mention on the day before, the event at the aquarium seemed to have faded from her mind. Yet a nervous edge had come into her activity level, whether from Friday's trauma or the prospect of her nanny's approaching departure, Brynn didn't know.

Clearing his throat, Michael continued, "But we talked about how your mother's gone to heaven and won't be coming back, didn't we?"

Jamie nodded.

"The part that's gone to heaven is her spirit, the part we can't see with our eyes."

Jamie squished scrambled eggs between the tines of her fork. "What's a spirit? Is it a ghost?"

"No, not exactly." He cast Brynn a look for help, but she wanted to hear what he'd say and smiled encouragingly.

"Well. It's all that made up your mother—her personality, her kindness, the love she had for you and the love she had for God."

"And the love she had for you," Jamie added.

His eyes flickered. "Right." He straightened his plate unnecessarily. "But there's a part of her here on earth that we honor by visiting sometimes."

"At the graveyard?" Jamie's tone was full of foreboding. "Where the ghosts live?"

"There are no ghosts, baby. Yes, at the cemetery, where we place a special stone telling about the person we love. And sometimes we bring flowers to decorate the grave. I thought today, after church, we'd go there and take your mother a bouquet of roses."

Brynn scarcely dared to breathe as she awaited Jamie's response. Whether he knew it or not, this was a positive move for Michael as well as his daughter, and she prayed Jamie wouldn't refuse.

What she didn't want to think about was how much he'd cared for his wife. Even though she'd known it all along, even though she reminded herself of it nine times a day, she still couldn't help feeling hurt by his loyalty.

She'd gone beyond thinking no one would ever love her that much. There was only one man she wanted to feel that strongly about her, and he was sitting across the table looking so appealing that all she could think about was nestling her cheek against his.

"Will she be able to smell the roses?" Jamie asked, bringing reality, sense and guilt back to Brynn in a rush.

"I don't know. Maybe she will at some level. Anyhow, it's a way to remember her that shows we love her."

"Huh," Jamie said, looking doubtful and afraid. Brynn squeezed her hand beneath the table.

Later, after Sunday school, Chad amused Brynn

by taking control for the church service. He couldn't hide his delight that Michael had accompanied them.

"This is called a bulletin," he pronounced gravely as he distributed a leaflet to each of them from the table in the narthex. "It helps you know how much longer we got to sit."

Michael thanked him and looked at Brynn with dry amusement.

The boy officiously led them down the aisle, announcing they always sat in the middle of church and near the end of the pew in case Jamie had to go to the bathroom. "Which," he assured them loudly once they were seated, "she always has to do, at least twice."

"I do not," Jamie retorted. "You do."

"Nah-uh. You."

"You're the one, silly."

"Hush," Michael said.

When they immediately fell silent, Brynn relaxed. It might be because they weren't as used to him, or it might be because he was a man, but the children never minded her that quickly. Having his support felt warm. It felt *good*.

She also liked seeing him share his hymnal with Jamie even though the child could read only a few words. Chad was just as fascinated. Although he kept his songbook open, he mouthed nonsense syllables while tilting his head to watch Michael, his penetrating soprano even more off-key than usual. Every now and then Jamie would make a face at him for his efforts. When Michael caught her at it, he tugged her chin back to the book, giving Chad a wink as he did.

The three of them were so wonderful Brynn wanted to fold them all in her arms and never let go.

Try as she might, she could register only one sentence in five of Pastor Duncan's sermon. He was an effective, earnest speaker, and she always left church with spiritual nuggets to ponder during the following week. But not today. Today her mind floated in clouds tinged pink with happiness and utter distraction.

After the service, even though a number of members made a point of welcoming Michael, her tension returned as she worried about how Jamie would react to seeing her mother's grave. The pastor was particularly warm. Brynn had a hard time meeting the good reverend's eyes for fear he'd noticed her inattention from the pulpit. But he was just as gracious as usual, and Michael responded pleasantly, if guardedly.

Bored, the children ran ahead to the van, and she had Michael to herself briefly as they followed.

"You know," she said, her manner hesitant, "I think it's very much for the best that you're going to Genna's grave. But are you sure you want Chad and me along? Maybe the two of you should be alone the first time."

"You're afraid."

"No, it's not that…yes, I guess I am, a little."

"Me, too. That's why I want you with us."

"Oh." She couldn't argue with that. To be needed by him felt satisfying beyond anything she knew.

When Michael drove beneath the arched iron entryway of Sherwin Memorial Gardens and down the narrow lane leading into the cemetery, Chad said, "Man. This must be where the rich people go to die."

Although Michael protested that most of Sherwin Falls' deceased were buried here, Brynn could understand the child's awe. Several well-maintained lanes branched off the main one to divide the cemetery into sections. Thanks to a generous sprinkler system, the grounds glowed a brilliant green. The tombstones in the older section were kept free of weeds and the flat headstones of the newer divisions appeared polished. Beautiful old oaks dripping with moss sheltered the bricked pathways between rows, and tasteful statuary centered several small seating areas. Everything was designed to signal rest, dignity and peace. Even the mausoleum avoided the cold look of many such structures, the rosy brick exterior designed to resemble a Federal mansion.

While they exited from the van, Brynn saw a family with teenaged children meandering down one of the pathways. An older gentleman wearing an elegant black suit, his stiff posture suggesting a military background, carried a bouquet of violets in the opposite direction. She wondered about them all, wondered if they mourned loved ones who had lived long, full lives or short, tragic ones like Genna's.

Michael removed a bundle of roses from the back of the van, took Jamie's hand and led them toward an area called "Promise." Brynn was careful to hold

Chad back, although he clearly resented it. When Michael paused before one of the graves and looped his arm across Jamie's shoulders, Brynn stopped and whispered to Chad that they should give them privacy.

"Why doesn't Mommy have a big stone like those over there?" Jamie asked, her tone plaintive and loud. Chad wriggled his hand from Brynn's and stepped closer. Brynn followed him without protest, feeling drawn as well.

Michael murmured something about the difficulty of mowing grass, then handed the roses to her. "Do you want to put them in the vase?"

The girl accepted the flowers without appearing to notice. "What does it say on the words?"

Chad made the final few steps to join Jamie, leaving Brynn to complete the foursome with an apologetic look for Michael. He didn't appear to mind; he merely pulled his daughter a step to the side to allow them room to make a semicircle around Genna's grave.

"I'll tell you, because I can read," the boy bragged. "Gen-na El-el—"

"Elyse," Michael supplied.

"Genna Elyse Wade Hudson, January 20, 1966– December 22, 1998, beloved wife and mother, rest with God and His angels."

"Mommy's under here?" Jamie quavered. "Under this ground?"

Michael clutched her nearer. "Only the portion that belongs to the earth. But remember when we talked about her spirit this morning. That's the important part of anyone, and your mother's spirit is with God. He's keeping her happy and safe until we can be with her again.''

Hearing a break in his voice, Brynn longed to give comfort, to put her arms around him as he did his daughter, but she didn't dare.

''That's not right!'' Jamie asserted. ''She don't belong in the earth, she belongs with me!''

''I know, baby,'' Michael said. ''But sometimes things don't work out the way we think they should.''

''Oh, Jamie,'' Brynn said, and though she dared not show her empathy for Michael, she couldn't resist doing so for the child. Moving quickly to Jamie's other side, she knelt on the grass and wrapped an arm around her waist. ''That's how I felt when my mother died. But after a long time I came to understand I had to accept she was gone. It helped when I thought of her living in heaven and enjoying a strong, healthy body while serving God. It still helps.''

''I don't remember my momma,'' Chad said. ''At least yours has got a better grave. I went to see Momma's once, but that's all, because she's way up in Michigan. She has this old plate with just her name and dates and stuff. Nothing about angels.''

Jamie stared at him with glassy eyes that tore at Brynn's heart.

After a long silence, Michael reminded her gently, ''Why don't you put the flowers in the vase.''

The girl glanced at the roses as if seeing them for the first time. Slowly she knelt and arranged them, then looked at her father.

"They'll die without water."

"The little container for the roses already has water in it."

"But in a while it'll run out."

"Yes, it will," he said, and stooped to rest a knee on the ground.

Less than a foot away, Brynn looked from his face to the child's. They were very intent on each other, and she felt privy to a moment sacred in its importance. She wanted to weep until she ran out of tears, but she knew she had to remain quiet, remain strong.

"And then they'll die," Jamie said.

Michael sighed. "That's right."

"But you can buy more," Chad encouraged. "There's always baby roses being born, and they're always beautiful."

Jamie's gaze moved to Chad. "But they're not the same ones."

"No, but they're good, too. Aren't they, Mr. Hudson?"

Brynn watched as Michael's eyes slowly found the boy's. She was surprised at the deep gentleness she saw there—surprised and hopeful.

Love him, she wanted to say. *How can you not love this child?*

"That's right," he said, and tousled the boy's hair. "All of God's creation is beautiful."

After a moment Jamie asked, "Can we bring daisies next week?"

Visibly brightening, Michael said, "Of course we can."

"Okay." With a serious expression, Jamie turned from her mother's grave and began walking toward the car, pulling her father with her. A deep weight lifted from Brynn's shoulders as she sent Michael a tiny smile. She meant to find Chad's hand as they followed Jamie, but managed to find Michael's as well.

The four of them together. It felt so right.

Chapter Sixteen

Brynn held back from telling Chad her adoption plans until she could meet with a lawyer, not wanting to raise his hopes unnecessarily. The earliest she could schedule an appointment was the middle of the following week. Over the weekend Mrs. Boyd had begun packing her clothing and Chad's, and Brynn had helped when she could. The old lady intended to keep only a few personal possessions in her new home, saying she didn't need much.

Mrs. Boyd left Chad with a neighbor on the afternoon she and Brynn visited the lawyer, Mr. Turnmeier, who questioned them thoroughly in his rustic office decorated with cowboy hats and black-and-white photos of Tennessee walking horses.

Given the unusual situation, Brynn couldn't mind that the elderly gentleman was cautious, though it was hard not to resent him thinking she was making a serious decision in haste. She did her best to convince him she was neither flighty nor childish.

After she had explained about her own passages through foster homes, he gave her a direct look over his bifocals, his watery eyes unimpressed, his expression telling her he'd seen a lot in his day and she was small potatoes.

"Are you certain you're not trying to relive your past through this boy, young lady? Trying to give him the stability you missed?"

She considered it. "I don't think so, but if I were, would that be so bad?"

"It would if you decide you've had enough in four or five years, when he's a six-foot-tall teenager mad at the world."

Yikes, she thought. Maybe it won't come to that. He might be shorter, and if it please the Lord don't let him be mad, at least not constantly.

She gave Mr. Turnmeier a wide grin, her heart bubbling with anticipation.

"Long before I knew Chad would need to find another home, from the first time I set eyes on him, I felt something special about the boy. Isn't that what love is all about, seeing the uniqueness in a person and loving them for it?"

The old man grunted. "I hope the boy sees something unique in you, then, and appreciates what he's got. We'll get started if that's what you both want, though it won't happen overnight. Since Mrs. Boyd has sole guardianship, she can sign the mother's affidavit and a few more papers. What we have to file is called an Independent Non-Relative Adoption. Now you will have sixty days to file for custody after all the release papers are signed.''

"I'm ready right now," she said.

His eyes narrowed. "How old are you?" When she told him, he said, "Just under the wire. You have to be twenty-five to adopt as a single person in Georgia. You said you were from Florida originally? How long have you lived here?"

"Since January."

"You can't file until you're a Georgia resident for six months."

That was disappointing. "I'll file that very day."

"After that, the court has sixty days between the filing and the hearing date during which time they'll appoint an agent of the court to investigate your past. Any skeletons in your closet?"

"I don't think so." This was getting more involved by the moment. She'd had no idea the legalities would be so complicated. "Is there a chance we'll go through all this and then the judge will deny custody?"

"If you check out okay, it's doubtful the judge will object. You'll be saving the state a whole wagonload of money."

Feeling comforted if impatient, Brynn helped Mrs. Boyd sign the papers, then assisted her to the van and back to her home.

Now all that remained was for Chad to be told, and she had a sudden burst of fear that he would object. After Mrs. Boyd was settled, she fetched him from next door and asked him to sit beside her on the front stoop.

When she announced her intentions, he was quiet for so long that she imagined the worst.

"Well, Chad? What do you think?"

"*You're* gonna adopt me?"

"Yes, if it's okay with you."

"I won't be going to live with strangers?"

"No, honey. You'll be right here in the same town, going to the same school."

"I'd be staying with you?"

"That's right," she said, laughing. His eyes were round as lollipops as he struggled to take it all in.

"Where, at Jamie's house?"

Her heart crimped to see the hope on his face. "No, I have a basement apartment in Marla Turner's home. She says she'd be glad to have a boy around the house. Do you know her, the kindergarten teacher?"

His disappointment was short-lived. "Oh, man! She was *my* teacher. Man! I'm gonna live with a bunch of *teachers!* Oh, no!"

"Is that a problem?" she asked anxiously.

"Nah, I guess not. I mean, I'll just have to make the best of it, like Grandma says." He beamed at her, and she couldn't resist giving him a quick hug. "When are we going to our new house? Now?"

"No, we'll have to wait until I finish the month of June with Jamie. I've promised to stay that long so they can find a replacement nanny." The words moved sluggishly from her lips as she thought of the girl's solemn face. "Your aunt has agreed to keep you until then."

"Oh, boring," he said. "But at least Grandma will be there."

"It won't be long before you can join me," she replied, and squeezed his shoulder even as her own spirits coiled downward.

No, it won't be long.

It won't be long before I have to leave Jamie and Michael.

Oh, Michael.

How was she going to bear it?

Over the next weeks, time abandoned its ordinary properties. Michael could lose himself in work for what seemed hours, only to find five minutes had passed. He might take a break and stare out his study window for a few moments, thinking, and when he looked at the clock he'd see half a morning had slipped by.

Somehow the days passed.

A spirit of change was in the air.

Jamie was restless and irritable, but less so when she found out Chad would continue to be a part of her life, although it caused some jealousy at first.

One evening he was approaching Jamie's bedroom to kiss her good-night when he overheard a conversation between his daughter and Brynn. Not meaning to eavesdrop, he stepped back from the door but couldn't prevent himself listening when he heard the topic.

"How come Chad gets to live with you and I don't?"

"You know why. His grandmother is sick and can't take care of him anymore."

"But I want to live with you, too."

"What, and abandon your beautiful daddy? Then he'd have to live all alone. You wouldn't want to make him sad, would you?"

"No," she answered, but she didn't sound too convinced.

Raising an eyebrow and reminding himself that eavesdroppers seldom heard good about themselves, he retraced his steps, then noisily approached the bedroom again.

On weekday afternoons he began interviewing candidates for the nanny position and received silent, reproachful looks from Barbara for his trouble. What did she expect him to do, keep Brynn here against her will? The woman had a mind of her own.

He winnowed the applications down to two. Both ladies were past sixty and had quiet, trustworthy personalities. He couldn't decide between them, though he was leaning toward the one with the Scottish accent. He enjoyed hearing her talk.

He needed something to lighten the misery churning inside.

Instead of hiring either, he postponed his decision and arranged for a week's vacation after Brynn left— to give Jamie and himself some time together before adjusting to another nanny. Maybe they'd go to the coast, walk along the beach, pick up some seashells.

Brynn acted as she always did, bright and optimistic, though he detected a pensive expression in her eyes now and then, especially when she looked at Jamie. At least she cared a little.

That wasn't fair. She cared a lot.

True to his word, he went to church with Brynn, Jamie and Chad on Sundays, even though it meant adding an hour's round trip to pick up the boy at his aunt's house.

Cedar West Bible had a more informal feel than the church Genna and he had attended, but he'd wanted a change anyway. Facing the questions at his old place after more than a year's absence had scant appeal, and he certainly didn't want the congregation speculating on his new "family."

Chad projected an air of self-importance every time he walked down the aisle beside Brynn, shadowing her as few biological children would. Seeing it, Michael found himself strangely moved.

Sometimes he thought he should reconsider and invite the boy into his life. That would provide an easy solution, if Brynn would have him.

But again, that wouldn't be fair, not to any of them. He couldn't take on Chad in order to marry Brynn. A child deserved to be viewed as more than baggage.

He *was* fond of the boy. Sometimes he wondered why he felt so set against adding Chad as a permanent member of the household. And then he thought of the complications he would cause. Jamie and he enjoyed a quiet, predictable, comfortable life. Chad would end all that.

Besides, every time he looked at the kid he remembered his own early, lost years.

He explained these things to himself over and over, yet still he felt uneasy.

Maybe that was why he allowed Brynn and Jamie to persuade him to participate in the parent-child softball game sponsored by several area churches.

"Didn't these ordeals used to be called father-son games?" he grumbled when asked over dinner on a Wednesday night near the end of June. Now he understood why Barbara had served fried chicken—to soften him up. He couldn't remember the last time she'd made it, having decided he was destined to die of a heart attack if he ate more than a tenth of his daily allotment of fat grams.

Lowering an ear of corn, Brynn met his eyes teasingly. "That would be politically incorrect, I believe."

"I thought churches didn't worry about things like that."

"Only when it matters," she said, smiling.

He found it hard to let go of her gaze, and he watched until her lashes fell.

"What's pol—pollick—what's that mean that you're talking about?" Jamie demanded.

"You remember the fairy tale about the emperor's new clothes?" he said, returning his eyes to Brynn. "It's something like that."

"Oh," Jamie said, sounding very wise. For a minute he felt a twinge of guilt for not explaining better, but then decided he'd done as well as he could.

Now, if Chad had been here, he wouldn't have let it go at that. The boy would have filled the air with talk, talk, talk.

Thinking it, looking from one hopeful pair of eyes to the other, he felt selfish and small. And so he agreed to take part in the game.

On the following Saturday morning Michael had cause to regret his decision when he donned his new red T-shirt stamped Cedar West's Best of the Nest. Cute how it rhymed, but the slogan wouldn't pass any marketing manager in his or her right mind. He pulled on the required white shorts and red cap, then viewed himself in the mirror. Ridiculous.

Funny how well the outfit looked on Brynn, though, and Jamie and Chad. The boy couldn't hide his pride as they entered the city's baseball complex. Over and over he bragged at passersby wearing other colors that the Nest would beat the rest. Michael finally had to ask him to stop.

"Okay, but I was just warning them," the boy said.

Why am I here? Michael wondered. This is Brynn's last weekend. I wanted to take her out to dinner, just the two of us.

Chad tugged on his arm. "Look at those pink shirts over there. They're just a bunch of babies, girl babies. We'll beat them, won't we?"

"Yeah, we'll beat them," Jamie said, running alongside.

"Not you, but us *guys*," Chad said, and shocked Michael by seizing his hand.

Brynn jogged a few paces in front and pretended to be irritated. "Excuse me, but we *girls* are going to make all the difference."

"Yeah!" Jamie chimed in.

Chad's fingers fluttered moistly within his hand. The boy hadn't moved without thinking, Michael realized. He'd made a purposeful gesture of affection and was probably regretting it, thinking he'd be rejected. Instinctively Michael tightened his fingers around the small hand.

"That's right," he said to Chad. "Remember we're all on the same team." His eyes sought Brynn's. "You don't want to be *politically incorrect.*"

"Okay," the boy said cheerfully.

Looking confused, Jamie said, "I don't see anybody without any clothes on."

Chad sputtered, "Of course you don't! Haven't you ever been to a softball game before? Did you think we was going skinny-dipping?"

Michael and Brynn burst into laughter. Maybe the day wasn't going to be so bad after all.

In the first round, Cedar West was paired against Hollow Grove Baptist on Field Three. The rounds were limited to three innings, and every position was manned by an adult and child.

Halfway through the second inning, Michael and

Chad took their turn at bat. The rules stated that children went first, so Chad seized the bat and scowled at the pitcher, a teenaged girl who appeared totally unimpressed. Nevertheless, her first pitch went high, and Chad let it sail by.

"Ball one!" yelled the umpire.

"Way to go, Chad," Michael encouraged as they exchanged places, and he was treated to a surprisingly modest smile.

"Hit it out of the park!" Brynn called to him from the dugout.

"Hit it out of town!" Jamie added.

"Hit it to the moon!" Chad shouted.

Michael gave them a solemn nod, lifted his bat and got into position. By this time the girl's father had bounded to the pitcher's mound and was comically licking his finger to test wind direction.

This whole thing might have been fun and games to everyone else, but Michael had become mysteriously involved in the competition and wouldn't allow the man in the green shirt to distract him. When the softball glided toward him, however, he saw it was going high and had to fight the impulse to hit it anyway.

It's a game, just a game. You don't have to prove anything. Give Chad another chance at bat.

Stifling a sigh of regret, he allowed the opportunity to pass by his right ear.

"Strike one," said the umpire.

Michael swerved instantly. "What?"

Catcalls and whistles sounded from the dugout and the scattering of people in the stands.

"Yeah, it went high, don't you know anything?" Chad challenged the adolescent boy in umpire's gear belligerently.

The umpire was giving the boy a scornful stare.

"Stee-rike wha-a-n," he repeated.

Chad knotted his fists and strode toward him.

Michael clamped his hand on the child's shoulder. "Your turn," he said.

"But he—"

"He's the umpire, and we need to show good sportsmanship."

"Even if he doesn't?"

"That's right."

Chad narrowed his eyes and nodded curtly. Michael stepped back as the boy took his place.

The girl pitched, and this time Chad connected, hitting the ball into left field. Michael grabbed his hand and pulled him toward first base, then second and third as the ball followed ineptly, slowed by four-handed fielders and players arguing over jurisdiction.

Just as they touched third, another toss went awry. The dugout went wild. Impressed by how well the boy had run but unsure what he had left, Michael asked, "Should we go for home?"

"Go!" the boy panted.

Without hesitation Michael jerked him forward. Chad kept up for a few steps, then staggered. Michael steadied him and slowed his pace, but although the boy struggled on gamely, he'd clearly run out of gas. My fault, trying to pull him too fast, Michael thought.

"Sorry," Chad cried as the ball sped past them toward home.

"No problem," Michael said, then felt a burst of hope as the catcher fumbled the ball. "Come here, guy." Moving smoothly, he lifted the child in his arms and barreled toward home.

An instant before the catcher tagged them, Michael's expensive athletic shoes touched home plate, and Chad slid downward to raise his arms in a victory dance that astonished Michael for its energy.

He viewed him narrowly, wondering if the child had been faking.

But it didn't matter. They were heroes in the dugout, and Brynn's enthusiastic hug was all he wanted out of the day.

"That was the prettiest home run I've ever seen," she said when the excitement died down and he sat beside her on the end of the bench. The other players had turned their attention to the next batter, and Chad was giving Jamie batting lessons a few feet away.

There was no point in denying it anymore. He'd tried to fool Andy, he'd held himself back with Brynn, but most of all he'd struggled to dupe himself. He loved Brynn and had loved her for a long time, maybe since the first day she walked into his office.

"You want to talk about pretty, look in the mirror."

Color flooded her skin, making her even more beautiful. "You're just trying to give me confidence for my turn at bat."

"You've found me out."

"Yes, only it's not working. You were fast. And strong, to run with Chad like you did."

"Check me at the end of the day. If I'm still walking, that's the real test."

"He looked so natural with you," she said softly. "Like you belonged together."

She never gave up. Michael studied her quietly, his gaze wandering from her smooth forehead and ash-colored brows to flawless cheeks. He avoided looking at her lips, knowing he would kiss her in front of God and a thousand witnesses if he did. He fought an urge to say he'd adopt the boy if she came with the deal.

Well, why not?

He knew why not—because he hadn't planned his future that way.

For too long his life had been full of complications, almost all in the form of people. Middle age was looming ahead of him like an ill-tempered, pondering bear. At this stage of his life he needed peace, and now that Jamie was coming to terms with her mother's death, there was a chance he could have it.

"I thought you'd decided he belonged with *you*," he said.

For an instant something moved in her eyes, and then she smiled faintly. "We do belong together."

I think *we* belong together, he longed to say.

"Brynn, have you really thought through what you're doing? No, no, don't look at me like that, I'm not accusing you of being too young anymore or of making quirky decisions. But you're a beautiful woman. Someday you'll want to get married, and Chad's going to hold you back. How many men do you think are willing to take on ready-made families?"

Anger flashed in her eyes. "I've told you how I feel about marriage."

"Yes, but that's *now*," he said, trying to bank down his own annoyance. "You've got a lifetime ahead of you. Somewhere along the way you might find someone who changes your mind."

"If that happens," she said, turning her profile to him, "he'll have to love Chad, too."

"All right, all right. Forget marriage for just a minute—"

"Forget marriage?" she said pertly. "I'm not even thinking about it. You're the one who brought it up."

"Even if you decide to stay single," he said in a steady voice, determined not to let his exasperation shine through, "what about your own rights?"

"My rights?" She looked as though she'd never heard of the concept.

"Yes, you know—your right to go where you want to go and when you want. To spend your money on a new car when you need it instead of buying school clothes or saving for college. You're a teacher, Brynn. That was your choice, and I know you're savvy enough to realize you're not going to have much money for extras. What if you want to go on a vacation to Europe? What if you get sick and can't take care of Chad anymore?''

Lost in the steady regard of her eyes, he finally ran out of steam.

"What if you get sick and can't take care of Jamie?" she asked softly. "What if you want to go somewhere but Jamie's appearing in a school play? If you complete your dream neighborhood, would you ever *really* try to finance it knowing you might lose everything and leave Jamie destitute?''

He swallowed. "That's different."

"Why? Because Chad didn't arrive in this world through my physical body? Weren't you the one telling Jamie it's the spirit of a person that really matters, not the part that's from the earth?''

He would have answered if he hadn't been so distracted by the earnest expression in her eyes, but at the moment he couldn't think of anything to say. He'd come up with something in a little while. Probably.

He shouldn't resent her for dashing his spun-sugar fantasies about the three of them making a family. Especially when she didn't know how he felt, though he doubted it would have made any difference if she did, determined as she was to provide a home for Chad. And he certainly wasn't going to ask her to make a choice between them. He loved her too much to put her in that position.

His gaze drifted toward Chad and Jamie. They had abandoned the batting efforts and were playing catch.

He noticed how carefully the boy aimed for Jamie's hands, how gently he threw.

And how loudly he corrected her when she missed.

One side of his mouth tugged upward in spite of himself. And then he was pleasantly surprised when Brynn rested a hand on his shoulder.

"You're talking about comfort," she said. "But when I weigh my own personal comfort against the chance of being part of Chad's life, there's no contest. I love him."

"I know you do," he said, his eyes skittering from her lips back to the children. His heart was pounding. He could understand why she loved him. It would be easy to love Chad. In his weaker moments he thought he already did.

But opening his heart to yet another complication would increase his vulnerability to the possibilities of hurt, of loss, of death. He was willing to risk that pain with Brynn, because he knew he loved and adored her, knew his life was going to be barren without her.

But Chad, too?

I want to, but I can't. I want to, but I can't.

"He's a very lucky little boy," he said, his voice sounding raw as he swung his gaze back to Brynn. "Lucky to have you."

Chapter Seventeen

The night before Brynn was to leave, Michael dreamed he was a boy again, camping on the Alaskan tundra with a group of Scouts. Chad was among them, helping him set up his tent, then sliding off behind a dogsled to an icy lake where they hammered holes and dangled lines for fish. Then in one of those incomprehensible dream shifts, Chad started drifting away from him on an ice floe, his face inexpressibly sad as he waved goodbye.

Michael awoke in a cold sweat.

As soon as he caught his breath, he rolled to his side in disgust. Talk about blatant symbolism. His brain wasn't very subtle.

It didn't matter. His subconscious mind would calm down in a week or two, he was certain of it.

And then the morning of Brynn's departure arrived.

He sat in his study with the door cracked and heard her telling Barbara goodbye, a tearful parting complete with a hug from the sound of it, all accompanied by the low, incessant moans of his daughter.

As he tapped his mechanical pencil against the desk, he imagined her stooping to Jamie's level and embracing her.

"Don't forget I'm coming back tomorrow to take you to the park," Brynn said.

"But you won't be here tonight," Jamie cried. "Or tomorrow night or ever again."

"No, but you'll be at the beach in two days. You and your dad will have the best time!"

"I won't, either!" Jamie wailed.

Michael threw down the pencil, stalked from the room and grabbed Jamie from Brynn's arms. Hugging her tight against one shoulder, he extended his right hand toward Brynn. She looked at it as if wondering what it was, then slowly shook his hand.

"We'll miss you," he said briskly.

"And I'll miss you." Her ravaged eyes moved from him to Jamie to Barbara. "All of you."

Barbara said, "See you later, dear," in a broken voice and rushed toward the kitchen.

"You sure you don't need the van today?" he asked, staring at a point a couple of inches over her head.

"No, you were very helpful last night. All my stuff is moved and my car's been trustworthy ever since I had it repaired." She reached out and touched Jamie's back, then finished thickly, ''So I guess I'll be off.''

He searched for words. ''Drive carefully,'' was all he could find.

''I will,'' she said, moving toward the front door. ''Thank you for everything.''

Without looking at her, he said, ''And we thank you.''

While she fumbled with the latch and Jamie's sobs increased in volume, he strode down the hall toward the kitchen. No way was he going to watch her leave.

Barbara was sitting at the kitchen table wiping her eyes with a paper napkin. She looked up in shock when he handed Jamie to her.

''I can't deal with this right now,'' he announced, and swerved toward the hall.

''Michael Joseph Hudson,'' she said commandingly.

Reluctantly he turned back and saw that, while she had wrapped her arms around Jamie, her eyes were sharp and disapproving.

''What?''

They locked gazes, his expression as forceful and stubborn as hers.

After what seemed hours, she said, ''I've seen how you look at Brynn. I've watched how you've treated her these past months. I believe I know what you feel for her. Are you going to let that wonderful girl get away?''

She kept watching him, while his blood rose to the boiling point. And now Jamie was craning her head to look, not understanding anything except that Barbara was on her side.

And then, quick as an Arctic plunge, his temper cooled as he suddenly thought, How empty the house sounds already.

Like flipping through a ghostly photo album, he saw the future as it should be: Jamie and Chad growing up together, companions and worst enemies trying out for sports teams, Brynn and himself carting them off to soccer games, Christmas plays, school events, piano lessons, both children growing tall and healthy and secure, inside and out, while Brynn and he drew closer, their lives twining like vines around a solid oak, them growing old together as their love for each other and God made them inseparable, made them one.

"No," he said angrily, and the anger was directed toward himself this time, "I'm not."

He dashed from the kitchen, up the hall and out the front door. The day was brilliant outside, the air calm and already hot. Brynn had nearly reached the end of the drive, her funny old car shaking, its engine running loud and sounding irritated. In a second she would turn onto the street and be gone. He could drive to her apartment, but it seemed crucial to stop her before then.

"Brynn!" he yelled, and took off down the drive.

She couldn't hear him, of course, and there was no need for her to look in her rearview mirror, not in a private driveway. She drove to the street and paused, looking one way, then the other.

He sprinted toward her. *Don't let the brake lights go off, don't let them go off!*

They went off. As the engine revved forward, his heart fell to his stomach.

Then the lights went on again. He saw her lean forward, put a tissue to her eyes and check her mirror.

He waved like a gorilla, trying to get her attention. Why was his driveway so long?

As she fiddled with the mirror, he squinted his eyes, watching her. Just like a woman, she only seemed to see herself. And then he saw her freeze, do a double take, then glance over her shoulder with a look of astonishment.

"Yes, it's me!" He laughed, still running.

She put her car in Reverse and backed a few yards, then stopped again. By the time he reached her, she'd rolled down her window, and he leaned on it to catch his breath. No doubt about it, he needed to start visiting the gym.

"What's wrong?" she asked anxiously.

"Turn off your engine," he panted.

"Why?"

"Because I want to talk with you."

Although she appeared unwilling, she did as he asked. "Is something the matter with Jamie?"

"I don't want to talk about Jamie right now. Get out of the car."

"What?"

He grinned. "Just get out of the car. Please."

Looking doubtful, she emerged from the vehicle.

Hardly had she put both feet on the ground when he pinned her with a long, slow kiss.

She pushed him away, blinking through a fresh crop of tears. "What are you *doing?*"

"I thought that would be the fastest way to tell you that I love you and don't want you to leave."

Anger flitted through her eyes. She gave his chest another gentle shove and walked several paces away, turning in a complete circle.

"How can you do this to me?"

"Do what, love you? It's easy!" While she glared at him, he added, "I know this seems sudden, but I've loved you for a long time. I lied to myself about it, but I can't lie anymore." He gestured toward the car. "This wasn't in the plan. I wanted to take you out to dinner, to spend a few months romancing you like you deserve. I wanted to win you over slow and easy, but circumstances have sped things up. I understand this is all a shock to you and you probably don't return my feelings, but do you think you could someday? Someday soon, I mean?"

She strode close to him, stared directly into his eyes, then backed away, her face softening into amazement.

"But that's not possible! You can't love me."

"And why not?" he asked indignantly.

"Because you loved your wife so much!"

"Are you trying to tell me a person can't love two people in one lifetime?"

"No, of course not, but I know how you are. You'll never love anyone as you did Genna. She was incredibly beautiful and kind. She was *unforgettable*. You said yourself she couldn't be replaced.''

''The same could be said of you.''

''But I'll never measure up. No, no, Michael. This can't work. You're lonely, anyone could understand that, and you'd like to have a mother for your child. You're a gentle man, a loving father. Naturally you want to provide a normal family life for Jamie. But this isn't the way, not with me. It would tear me up inside, feeling as if I were always taking second place to Genna. I know that sounds selfish of me, but there it is.''

''You could never take second place to anyone.''

''That's easy to say, and I appreciate that you're trying to soothe my feelings, but—''

''Brynn, I have never met anyone I loved as much as you.''

''—but it won't work, and...what?''

The hope in her eyes made him want to laugh out loud. ''I loved Genna, there's no denying that, but our relationship wasn't what I wanted it to be.''

She swallowed, looked at the hedge, then back at him.

''It wasn't?''

''This is hard for me to say because it sounds disloyal. Genna was a child in many ways. She had a thousand fears. She worried excessively about Jamie, to the point of overprotection, and was convinced I'd die and leave her alone. It was hard for her to make the smallest decision without consulting me first.''

After the first year, the charm of her dependency

had worn thin, had nearly strangled him in fact, but he wouldn't tell Brynn that. Maybe someday he'd let her know that in those last months before the accident he'd come to feel his marriage to Genna was a mistake, but not now.

He doubted Brynn could understand how impatient he'd become with his wife, how he'd come to dread a future with a woman too insecure to drive herself into town. Brynn might sense his guilt ran deeper than it appeared, but she didn't need to know how deep.

Genna's death had not been his fault; he knew that. But he was guilty just the same. Guilty for not loving her as much as she needed when she was alive.

All of that he'd save for another day. Right now he had to mow down Brynn's early insecurities and mend the tears in her spirit inflicted by her ex-fiancé.

Somehow he had to convince her she was the most wonderful woman in the world, because she was.

"You, on the other hand, are able to think for yourself. You're intelligent and sensitive and warm, sometimes stubborn—but I like stubborn—and I look forward to a lifetime of equal partnership with you."

"And with God?"

"Him most of all, because I'm guessing He's the one who arranged all of this. So what do you say? I know this is all news to you and you'll need some time to think. We can go out, date like a couple of kids if you want, while you consider whether or not you could take on Jamie and me permanently...."

Her eyes growing moist, she approached him so

solemnly that he didn't know what she intended until she lifted her face to his. He kissed her more than willingly, then was dismayed when she broke away too soon.

"I love you, Michael, and no amount of dating could make me more convinced. But I have to think about Chad."

"I know. He's welcome, too."

"But you were absolutely against it before!"

"Can't a man change his mind?"

"Are you sure? Have you thought it all out? Because if you resent him, you'll come to resent me, too."

He cupped her chin in his hand. "There's no doubt in my mind he's going to be a challenge to us both. Physically, mentally, probably spiritually, too. But as my mom used to say, nothing worthwhile ever comes easy."

He kissed the tip of her nose. "Besides, a few minutes ago I remembered the extraordinary way he came into our lives, and that's when it occurred to me that our love isn't only about you and me and Jamie. It's about him, too."

"Oh, Michael," she said, her eyes glistening like moonlight on water. "Small miracles at work again, bringing us all together."

"Not so small, my love," he said, folding her into his arms. "Not small at all."

Epilogue

Two years later

"Look what we found, Mommy," Jamie said, climbing down the path to the flat rock where Brynn had spread a blue-checked tablecloth and was unloading a picnic lunch. The girl moved awkwardly because of the writhing golden bundle she held in her hands.

Brynn straightened, her hand going to her back in a gesture becoming more automatic by the day. "Another puppy?"

"Somebody abandoned him," Jamie said, her words nearly absorbed by the roar of the falls. "Look how cute he is."

The shivering animal, hardly bigger than Jamie's two hands, met Brynn's gaze for an instant then looked away, his chocolate velvet eyes pitiful and lost.

"Oh, brother," she said, and had to laugh. "You already have a dog."

"That's what I told her," Michael said, descending toward them from the path. "Enough is enough."

He looked far too innocent, Brynn thought.

"It wasn't my idea," Chad said, scrambling over the edge. "She'll feed him two days and then I'll have to do it, just like I have to take care of Biscuit."

"I will too feed him and brush him and take him for walks, just like you do Biscuit because Biscuit's your dog!"

Brynn gave Michael a long, probing look. His eyes moved from the falls to the river to the lunch spread invitingly on the rock, everywhere but at her. Taking an expansive breath, he said in a satisfied voice, "Well, it looks as if the food is ready!"

"Um-hmm," Brynn said knowingly, a smile tugging her lips. "The food is ready, all right."

They sat on the cloth, Michael rushing to help Brynn sit on the folding chair they'd brought just for her. Two more months and she wouldn't be so awkward anymore. Two more months and Michael Patrick Hudson would be born. They planned to call him Pat for Brynn's father. She couldn't wait.

God had been so good to them.

After grace, they passed bologna sandwiches, deviled eggs and the rest, then began to eat, their conversation centering on the dog, who was offered his own sandwich, carefully torn into tiny pieces by Jamie.

Brynn, lost in memories, didn't say much.

This rock, once so sacred to her because of her mother, had become their family's special place, for it was here she had married Michael almost two years ago.

It had been a small wedding with only a few special friends and relatives invited. Mrs. Boyd, in a remission that continued to this day, had felt well enough to attend. The pastor of Cedar West Bible officiated, and Jamie and Chad had served as their attendants. Michael's brothers and their families, relationships renewed, also came, as had Barbara and Andy.

She hadn't worn the bridal gown she'd chosen for her wedding with Reed; that was long gone, sold through a newspaper ad before she moved to Georgia. Instead she'd purchased an ivory tea-length dress that she could wear again at elegant functions.

But she *had* unpacked the bridal veil she'd saved, and had asked the florist to arrange wildflowers, not the rosebuds she'd planned for Reed, around the headpiece. When she pinned it carefully in her hair, she felt that special connection she'd known would come. Her mother had worn it first, over thirty years ago. Looking at her image in the mirror, Brynn had felt certain her parents were watching her, too, with approval.

Feeling Michael's hand touch her arm, she returned to the present. "Are you uncomfortable?" he asked.

He would never know how much. She smiled and said, "I'm fine."

"So, what about the puppy?" Jamie asked.

Michael, his eyes lingering on Brynn, said, "We have enough excitement in our house already. We're not running an animal shelter, for crying out loud."

"See, I told you," Chad grumbled.

Brynn rested her hand over Michael's. "We'll keep him."

As the children crowed in delight, she gave her husband a secret smile when he kissed her cheek and asked if she was sure.

"You're an architect," she said, paraphrasing the wedding vows they had written and exchanged at this special place. "You should know by now how to build a family. One precious life at a time."

"Built on a foundation of love," he added, moving closer.

"And nurtured by God," she said, and leaned forward for his kiss.

* * * * *

Dear Reader,

As part of the baby-boomer generation, I've been alive long enough not to be young anymore, although it pains me to admit it. But growing older (not *old* quite yet, I hasten to add) has a number of advantages that aren't readily apparent when counting the latest wrinkles in the mirror.

One of those advantages is perspective.

When something bad happens to us in childhood, whether catching chicken pox the day before the class trip, or something even more serious, the natural response is, "Why did this happen to *me*? It's not *fair!*"

A teen may or may not react in the same manner, depending on maturity level.

By the time we reach young adulthood, most of us have learned not to respond in such childish ways, at least not out loud.

By middle age and onward, we come to realize that everyone experiences tragedy in life, and that it's not how sadly my life compares with yours that's important, but how each of us is able to deal with our own particular losses.

Unfortunately, some folks never stop feeling singled out by misfortune and bear the inevitable consequences inside: bitterness and depression and isolation.

In this novel, Brynn and Michael both experience harsh blows in life that seem impossible to bear. As they learn to look outside themselves and to the One who heals all wounds, I hope you will find encouragement on your own faith journey.

Lovingly,

Marcy Froemke